Trial by Fury

Widowed Constance Lawley rather enjoyed
taking occasional domestic jobs to help out in
other people's family crises. She enjoyed the
beginning of the week she spent with Colonel
Barrow, whose wife was recovering from an
operation, and she was intrigued by their grandson, a strange, brilliant, unpredictable teenager.
But she had not bargained for the dramatic in-
crease which occurred in the family's crises, nor
that these would end in bloodshed.

The police regarded it as an open-and-shut
case—until another body turned up to invalidate
all their theories. In spite of herself, Constance
began to probe a little more deeply into the
Barrows' relationships and those of others in the
village where they lived. What she uncovered was
as unexpected as the extra body, but with her
daughter's help she began to make sense of it and
to realize that the crime was far more complex
than anyone had thought.

ELIZABETH FERRARS

Trial by Fury

COLLINS, 8 GRAFTON STREET, LONDON W1

William Collins Sons & Co. Ltd
London · Glasgow · Sydney · Auckland
Toronto · Johannesburg

First published 1989
© M. D. Brown 1989

British Library Cataloguing in Publication Data

Ferrars, Elizabeth
   Trial by fury.—(Crime Club)
   I. Title
   823'.912[F]

ISBN 0 00 232120 3

Photoset in Linotron Baskerville by
Rowland Phototypesetting Ltd
Bury St Edmunds, Suffolk
Printed in Great Britain by
William Collins Sons & Co. Ltd, Glasgow

CHAPTER 1

The telephone rang.

Constance Lawley reached for it and said, 'Yes?'

'Mrs Lawley,' a woman's voice said.

'Yes,' Constance said again.

'Are you free at the moment?' the voice asked. 'For another job, I mean.'

'Oh dear,' Constance said. 'I've only just got home. I was hoping for a week or two to myself.'

'Well, if you can't, you can't. How was that last job?'

'Not bad, I suppose. They were nice people. But they wouldn't eat vegetables that hadn't been organically grown or eggs that weren't free range. They may be right about all that sort of thing, for all I know, but it did make life complicated.'

'When did you get back?'

'This afternoon. And the first thing I did was buy myself a slab of fillet steak and I'm going to have it with some sauté potatoes and mushrooms. I couldn't look another salad in the face. And I've got a half bottle of Saint Emilion and I'm going to have a nice quiet evening.'

'You mean they were teetotal too?'

'Not exactly. We sometimes had a nip of dandelion wine. It was really quite good. And they were really very nice people, very appreciative of everything I did for them.'

What Constance Lawley had been doing for the people of whom she was talking was housekeeping for them, for a week after the wife of a retired solicitor in the town of Bracklington, where Constance lived, had returned from hospital after an operation for gallstones. For the last two years, since her husband had died and she had found her days long and empty, Constance had been working for an institution called the Bracklington Helpers, who supplied helpers of all sorts to people who, through illness or old age or calamities of other kinds, suddenly needed assistance in their houses. She seldom worked for more than a week for anyone, but while she did she would cook, wash up, shop, do some washing if that was needed and generally keep the house in order.

The pay was not high but she was interested in people and inclined to like more of them than she disliked, and the work, after all, was only what she had been doing for most of her life. She had married young a man who was fifteen years older than herself and they had had two children, one of whom, Peter, was now farming in New Zealand and the other, Irene, a girl of twenty-nine who Constance thought was old enough to know better, was doing something peculiar with a religious sect who were given to chanting in strange tongues and lived in a community in the East End of London.

Constance herself was sixty. She was a small, slim, vigorous woman with short, curly grey hair that had once been dark, large dark eyes in the glance of which there was a curious mixture of directness and diffidence, a smile that was usually amiable but could be sardonic, and a firm, pointed chin. Her husband had been a lecturer in economics in Bracklington Polytechnic and as she had his pension and was modest in her tastes, the fact that the Helpers did not pay her a great deal was not of the first importance.

'What was it you wanted me to do?' she asked.

'Just another housekeeping job,' the voice which belonged to Mrs Jay, who ran the Helpers' office for them, replied. 'But if you're tired—'

'Oh, I'm not tired,' Constance said. 'It's just that it feels nice to be at home. But if it's something urgent, perhaps I could do it. Where is it?'

'In Long Meldon.'

Long Meldon was a village about ten miles from Brack-lington.

'When would I have to go there?' Constance asked.

'Not until next Wednesday. Mrs Barrow—that's the woman's name—is coming out of hospital on Wednesday morning. She's had her appendix out. There's only herself, her husband and a grandson in the family.'

'A grandson? Then she's fairly old, is she?'

'About eighty, I think.'

'Isn't it very unconventional to have your appendix out at eighty? I thought it usually hit you fairly young or not at all.'

'I believe that's so. Anyway, she's had appendicitis and she's being sent home on Wednesday, and her husband's about eighty too, I believe. I'm not sure how old the grandson is.'

'What happened to his parents?'

'Killed in a car crash or something like that, I gathered. And the old man's been coping while his wife was in hospital, but he sounded a bit desperate on the telephone about managing to look after her once she's home. You know how quickly they push you out of hospital nowadays. Once you're no longer actually at death's door, out you go.'

'It isn't a nursing job, is it, because I'm not qualified for that.'

'No, I understand she's made a perfectly good recovery, it's just that she won't be up to the job of cooking and so on for a little while and her husband thinks that a diet of baked beans might not suit her. What about it, Mrs Lawley? Do you feel a bit tempted?'

One of Constance's failings was that she was very easily tempted to take on work of which, only a few minutes before the telephone had rung, she had felt so glad to be free. She thought of the old man and the young boy and the still frail and convalescent woman of eighty probably trying to cook for them before she was fit to do so, and she thought of her own comparative youth, being merely sixty, and all the energy that she had to spare, and that Wednesday was some days off.

'Well, perhaps I could,' she said indecisively, though her mind was really already made up.

'Good, good,' Mrs Jay said. 'I'm so glad. He sounded nice. He said he got the address of the Helpers from his doctor. You'll drive out there, I suppose. The address is Colonel Barrow, Riverside, Long Meldon, and the telephone number—'

'Wait a minute,' Constance interrupted. 'I must get a pencil and write it down . . . Yes, all right, what is it?'

'Long Meldon 850. And they'd like you to get there about twelve o'clock, if you can manage that. Mrs Barrow will be home by then.'

'Is it a very big house?' Constance asked. 'Is there any other help?'

'I'm not sure. Colonel Barrow sounded as if he and the boy had been managing on their own, so perhaps there isn't. But you'll really take it on, will you, Mrs Lawley? Can I telephone him and tell him it's fixed up?'

'Yes.'

'That's very good of you. Thank you so much. I can give him your number, can't I? I dare say he'll want to ring you up himself and confirm it.'

'Yes, of course.'

'Well, enjoy your steak.'

Mrs Jay rang off.

Constance put her telephone down and reached for the glass of sherry that she had just poured out when the telephone rang. She went through a brief spell, as was customary with her, of cursing herself for having accepted the job in Long Meldon when there were all kinds of things that wanted attention in her own house. If she did not get down to some thorough cleaning in it soon, it would be becoming squalid. For one thing she had been promising

herself for some time to dust all her books and only half an
hour ago had made up her mind to start on them next day.
But if she was leaving home again on Wednesday there were
a number of other things that she must see to first.

All the same, perhaps the job would be interesting. She
had never worked in an army family before and was inclined
to think of them as a peculiar species who might have all
sorts of strange habits and prejudices as unfamiliar to her
as the importance of organically grown vegetables had been
to her last employers. But Long Meldon was a pretty village
and life there would probably be easy and peaceful.

How impossible it is to look into the future.

At eleven o'clock on Wednesday morning she set off for
Long Meldon in her Mini. She had had the car for five years
and kept telling herself that it would really be an economy
to sell it and buy a new one before it entirely lost its value.
But she was used to it and even had a kind of affection for
it. Sometimes she went so far as to get estimates for other
somewhat newer second-hand cars, but when it came to the
point she could not persuade herself to write the necessary
cheque. Her little dark blue car very seldom gave her any
trouble and only fairly small repair bills. She had packed a
suitcase after breakfast, put it in the boot and presently
drove off through the sunny summer morning.

Long Meldon had once been a village of small, stone,
thatch-roofed cottages that straggled along a main road for
a fair distance, hence its name. The cottages had once been
lived in mainly by farm labourers, but now were mostly
inhabited by retired professional people from Bracklington,
or even from as far away as London, Manchester, Glasgow
and other points north, who had installed central heating,
dishwashers, second bathrooms and double glazing. Their
front doors were painted in a variety of bright colours and
some of them had flower baskets hanging from their porches.
There had once been meadows behind the cottages, but

these had now been built up with bungalows and council houses and the two old country pubs had been transformed into quite luxurious small hotels. There were a few shops and one garage. Crossing the road under the stone arch of a bridge that was in fact the oldest building in the village was the river Meldon, a lazy stream flowing between steep banks overhung by willows.

Constance had to stop her car and ask a passer-by where a house called Riverside was. She was told that she should cross the bridge, bear left, then turn into a small lane on the right and that the house she wanted was about a hundred yards up it. She followed these directions and found a gate with the name Riverside painted on it. The gate was open and she drove through it into a gravelled courtyard in front of a medium-sized stone house. Stopping the car opposite the solid-looking oak front door, she got out, took her suitcase from the boot, went up to the door and rang the bell.

After a moment the door was opened by a small, thin, bearded man whose age she guessed was, as she had been told, about eighty. In spite of his age, however, he did not stoop, holding himself as erect as a young man, and though his hair was white it had receded only a little from his high forehead. His eyes were blue, looking very bright in his deeply tanned, thin, wrinkled face. His beard was a small one, neatly trimmed. He was wearing an open-necked blue shirt, grey trousers and slightly earthy grey canvas shoes which gave him the look of just having come in from gardening.

He had spoken to Constance once on the telephone two days before, confirming that she would be coming to Long Meldon on the Wednesday morning, and she knew that he had a rather high-pitched, hurried way of speaking which suggested to her that he was a shy man, nervous of addressing a stranger.

'Mrs Lawley?' he said, holding out a hand. Its grasp felt rough, as if it was used to a good deal of hard work. 'It's so

good of you to come. My wife and I are immensely grateful.
It isn't that she's ill, you know, she's quite got over the
worst, only not quite the thing yet, and I'm sure you'll be
able to give her the kind of food she ought to have instead
of the rather awful things that are all that I can manage.
She says she doesn't mind what she has because she hasn't
any appetite anyway, but I'm sure we ought to tempt her
to eat, don't you think so? No—let me carry that.'

He reached quickly for Constance's suitcase as she was
about to pick it up. She felt, in view of his age, that she
ought to carry it herself, but he grasped it firmly.

'Come along,' he said. 'I'll show you your room first,
then you must come and meet Dorothea. I hope you'll be
comfortable, though I'm afraid the room's very small and
it hasn't got a television, but you must come and watch ours
whenever you want to. Have you any favourite programmes
that you specially like to watch? Don't hesitate to say so.
While my wife was in hospital Colin and I often watched
all kinds of programmes that we'd never have thought of
watching in the ordinary way, and really we sometimes
found some of them quite amusing. Colin's our grandson.
Of course it's school holidays now so he's at home, but you
won't find him any trouble.'

While he was chattering he was leading Constance to the
foot of a curving staircase and up it into a narrow passage.
The house, she guessed, was very old. She thought that it
had probably been built in the seventeenth century and
perhaps had once been a farmhouse. It was not big enough
ever to have been a manor, but was much larger than a
cottage and had been moderately, though not lavishly,
modernized. The windows that lit the passage were small,
with brightly patterned curtains, and the floor of wide
polished boards with a strip of red carpet along it, was
uneven. There were some thick beams in the walls.

The room into which Colonel Barrow took her was certainly small, with only a bed in it, covered with a pretty

patchwork bedspread, a built-in hanging cupboard, a chest
of drawers with an attractive old mirror standing on it, and
an easy chair. But opening a door which she had assumed
was part of the cupboard, he showed her with a touch of
shy pride that it opened into a little bathroom that she
would have to herself.

'But it's perfectly lovely!' she exclaimed.

'It's all right, you'll be able to manage, you'll be quite
comfortable?' he asked with a note of anxiety in his voice.

'If you'd seen some of the places I've stayed in!' she
replied. 'Now what can I do? I can unpack later. If you'll
show me the kitchen and so on I can start seeing to lunch.'

'No, you must come down and meet my wife and perhaps
have a glass of sherry with us,' he said. 'She isn't in bed,
you know, she gets up and sits in the drawing-room, or
sometimes out on the terrace if it's warm enough. She
wanted to do that today, but there's a little bit of a breeze
blowing and I thought it would be better for her to stay
indoors, don't you think so yourself? We don't want her
catching cold.'

Constance had thought the morning very beautiful, but
she answered, 'You may be right.' She was inclined, or at
any rate appeared to be inclined, to think that other people
were generally right. She disagreed with other people as
seldom as she could. This could lead at times, she was
aware, to hypocrisy, but on the whole it made life easier,
especially when you spent as much time as she did among
strangers.

The Colonel had set off briskly along the passage, leading
the way, then down the stairs and across a small, stone-
paved hall into a bright, attractive room beside the great
open fireplace of which a small, dumpy woman was sitting.

'My wife,' Colonel Barrow said. 'Mrs Lawley.'

He smiled at them both with the air of happily congratulating himself on having brought them together.

This he had actually done, since it had been he who had

somehow cleverly discovered, while his wife was still in hospital, that an organization called the Bracklington Helpers existed, and that they, if you were fortunate, would be able to send some kind woman to your home to look after it if you happened to be in trouble.

There were no obvious signs that Mrs Barrow was in trouble except for shadows under her eyes which perhaps were not normally there and a slight tightness of the mouth. But in a face as wrinkled as hers it was difficult to tell how much came from illness and how much simply from old age. Her eyes were grey and so was her hair which was drawn straight back from her small, oval face and twisted into a roll at the back of her head. She was wearing a gaily patterned cotton dress, no stockings and velvet bedroom slippers. Her bare legs showed some prominent veins. She sat slumped on a sofa and when Constance was introduced to her did not move except to hold out a small hand to her and to give her a small, singularly sweet smile.

'We're so grateful to you for coming,' she said. 'Not that we couldn't have managed by ourselves. My husband's making too much fuss of me. I'm really very well.'

'That's the problem,' Colonel Barrow said. 'Trying to stop her doing more than she ought. She isn't used to being ill. Now you'll have some sherry, won't you? Then we can discuss how we're going to arrange things.'

'You must tell us how you like to do everything,' Mrs Barrow said. 'We'll leave it all entirely to you. We aren't used to having a housekeeper. Of course when we were in India before the war we had quite a household. We had a cook and a boy and an ayah and a dhobi and a dersey and a sice, and I had absolutely nothing to do. You can't think how bored I used to get. Now we just have a very wonderful woman called Mrs Newcome who comes in twice a week to clean the house. She'll be coming tomorrow. You'll like her, she's so kind and efficient. But when it comes to deciding what to give us to eat, you must say what you want to cook and tell my husband what you want him to get from the shops, or he can show you where to go shopping yourself, if that's what you'd prefer.'

A feeling that she was in luck and might have a pleasant week ahead of her came over Constance.

Sitting down, accepting the glass of sherry that the Colonel brought to her, she said, 'But you must tell me how you like things done. For instance, what do you like to eat and what don't you?'

'Oh, we eat anything,' Mrs Barrow said. 'We really aren't difficult.'

'No allergies?' Constance said. 'Nothing I must be careful to avoid?'

'Not a thing,' the old man said as if the suggestion that he or his wife might have anything so outlandish as an allergy were faintly shocking. 'No, indeed. If you've travelled as much as we have, you can't afford to have such things.'

'Though there are some things we like better than others, that's true,' his wife said. 'But I don't think there's anything we couldn't eat if we had to.'

'But we don't much care for tripe,' Colonel Barrow said on a note of apology, as if he were afraid that Constance's only aim at the moment might be to hurry down to the butcher in the village and buy tripe in quantity.

'Nor octopus,' Mrs Barrow said. 'My husband was stationed in Italy for a time after the war and they were always giving us octopus. I could never really take to it.'

'And I don't like oysters,' a voice said behind Constance.

She started and looked round and saw the handsomest young boy whom she could remember ever having seen looking gravely at her.

He had come in through the french window that opened out of the drawing-room on to a terrace where there were garden chairs placed around a round white-painted table. There was a chessboard on the table with white and black chessmen standing about on it, as if the boy had been in

the middle of a game with himself when he had stopped it
to come in and take a look at Constance. The french window
had a modern look and must have been pierced through the
thick wall of the house not so very long ago, for it did not
match the little casement on the opposite side of the room,
or go with the low beamed ceiling and yawning old fireplace
in which logs had been neatly laid across the fire-dogs,
though naturally on such a fine August day had not been
lit.

The boy came forward. He was dressed in jeans and a
loose white shirt.

'Anyway you couldn't get oysters in Long Meldon even
if you wanted to,' he said reassuringly. 'They're still alive
when you eat them, you know. *Alive!* Just think of it. I'm
Colin.'

'Our grandson,' Colonel Barrow said.

Constance could not make up her mind about the boy's
age. He was about the same height as his grandfather,
slender like him and he moved with a compact kind of grace.
He had black wavy hair, cut so that it showed the perfect
shape of his head, dark eyes and delicately etched dark
eyebrows above them. His face was narrow and thin, with
a thin, high-bridged nose and a mouth that was on the
smallish side but with finely modelled lips. They smiled
pleasantly at Constance, showing regular, very white teeth
as he came forward and held out his hand to her. She had
a feeling that he was aware of how his looks probably
impressed her. She smiled back at him, placing him as
probably twelve or thirteen years old, though perhaps rather
old for his age. That might be a result, she thought, of his
having been brought up by grandparents instead of parents.
Yet even as she thought this, it seemed to her that there
was a certain strangeness about the boy, some of it due to
his astonishing good looks, but some of it to the almost fiery
intensity with which he looked at her.

It was a feeling that she was to remember later.

*

Drinking her sherry, she suggested that Colonel Barrow should show her the kitchen and that she could then proceed to produce some lunch, what it could be depending on what happened to be in the house. Then after it, she said, she could go to the village shops to choose something for the evening.

The Colonel held up a hand.

'No need,' he said. 'I thought that you wouldn't want to dash out shopping as soon as you got here, so the lunch, such as we're used to having, is out in the dining-room now. We never have much lunch. There's bread and cheese there and some fruit, peaches, bananas, that sort of thing, and you'll find the freezer's well stocked up with things I got from Marks and Spencer in Bracklington yesterday. I'll introduce you to the shops tomorrow.'

One of the problems that Constance often encountered in her work then showed itself. It was simply the question of whether she should eat with the Barrows in the dining-room or alone in the kitchen. The Barrows took for granted that she would eat with them, but she stuck to a principle that she had worked out for herself that it was far better to insist from the beginning that she would stick to the kitchen for her meals. For warm though her welcome might be when she first arrived in a household in need of her help, they might soon become tired of her company once they were used to her. Besides, she found it restful herself to eat comfortably in silence, without having to make the effort of conversing with people whom she hardly knew. That day, when Colonel Barrow had shown her the kitchen, which she was relieved to see had been satisfactorily modernized, with a dishwasher, refrigerator and other conveniences, and when she had been up to her room once more to unpack her suitcase, she sat down at the kitchen table, ate bread and cheese and reflected that she saw no serious problems ahead of her.

She began her work once lunch was over, clearing the dining-table and stacking the dishwasher, then because she had nothing special to do for the moment, yet felt restless in her new surroundings, she began to make a cake. Mrs Barrow, she knew, had gone upstairs to lie down while the Colonel had gone out to work in the garden. The boy, she thought, had returned to his interrupted game of chess. But presently, while she was beating the eggs and sugar for a sponge, he appeared at the kitchen door.

'Hallo,' he said diffidently, looking unsure if he would be welcome.

'Hallo,' Constance replied.

'What are you doing?'

'Making a cake.'

'Do you like making cakes?'

'Sometimes.'

'I'm going to have a cake for my birthday.'

'That sounds nice. When is it?'

'On Sunday.'

'How old will you be then?'

'Fifteen.'

It troubled her. She had decided that he was probably a rather sombre and dignified twelve-year-old, and now she had to think of him as a somewhat childish teenager.

He advanced into the kitchen.

'How long are you going to stay here?' he asked.

'A week, I think,' she said.

'Do you like it here?'

'I think I'm going to like it very much.'

'I don't much like it,' he said. His glowing eyes had been fixed intently on her face ever since he had appeared at the door. She began to have an uncomfortable feeling that in spite of their brilliance there was a certain emptiness in them. 'I've always lived here. My mother and father are both dead.'

'I'm sorry,' Constance said.

'You needn't be. I can't remember them. They were both killed when I was a baby.'

'In a car crash?'

'Something like that.'

It was said in a flat tone, as if it were a matter of no importance, yet it startled her.

'You mean you aren't sure . . .' But she stopped herself. The boy had said everything since he had come into the kitchen in the same tone and probably the matter really was of no importance to him.

'My mother was very beautiful,' he said. 'Everyone says so.'

If he had inherited his good looks from her, Constance thought, this could well be true.

'Was she the daughter of Colonel and Mrs Barrow,' she asked, 'or was your father their son?'

'Oh, she was their daughter,' he said.

'Then your name isn't Barrow,' she said. 'What is it?'

'It's Barrow. Of course it's Barrow.' He spoke with sudden excitement. 'I'm Colin Barrow.'

She nearly asked him if his parents had been first cousins. If they had, she thought, it might partly account for what was strange about their beautiful son, but she stopped herself, feeling that perhaps this would be getting into deep water.

'My father was no good,' he announced. 'Everyone says so.'

'Who are everyone?'

'Oh, Grandma and Grandpa. Do you play chess?'

The change of subject was so abrupt that she was fairly sure it was what he had come to the kitchen to ask her.

'I'm afraid I don't,' she answered. 'I'm not nearly clever enough.'

'You don't really have to be clever if you can find someone to play with who isn't a lot cleverer than you are. I play a lot with Conrad. I can generally beat him, but sometimes I think he lets me do it on purpose.'

'Who's Conrad?' She was folding flour into her sponge.

'He's a friend of ours. He lives just a little way up the lane, but he works in Bracklington. He's got a shop there.'

'What kind of shop?'

'He sells furniture and things.'

'Oh, Conrad Greer!' She recognized the name of one of the antique shops in an arcade in the heart of Bracklington. Most of the shops there were antique shops, or bookshops, or boutiques, or small, expensive jewellers. She could only very occasionally afford to shop there.

Colin nodded. 'Do you know him, then?'

'I think I've spoken to him,' she said. 'I once bought a little Chelsea bowl in his shop. I suppose it would be he who sold it to me.'

'He's very nice,' Colin said. 'I think he may be coming over to us later today because Wednesday's early closing day in Bracklington. I wish you played chess too.'

'I'm sorry I don't.' She slid her sponge into the oven and said, 'I do hope this will be a success. It's sometimes difficult to get it right with an oven you don't know.'

'I hope it will be too. Grandma's no good at cakes. Usually we just have chocolate biscuits for tea.'

He gave her the first warm smile that she had seen on his face and suddenly left the kitchen.

The sponge was a success and Constance found that dinner that evening had been so organized beforehand by Colonel Barrow that she had very little to do. She found a cooked chicken in the refrigerator and the makings of a salad and also a packet of ice-cream and a tin of peaches. Not an exhilarating meal and next day, she promised herself, she would provide something more interesting for the family, but for a first evening in the household, when she still hardly knew where to lay her hands on what she wanted, it was certainly convenient.

The Barrows were very insistent that she should join them again for sherry before dinner, and as she could not claim that she had any more to do just then than to lay the table, she accepted. Going into the drawing-room, she saw Colin outside on the terrace, seated at the table there, poring over the chessboard on it and with a man sitting facing him who at that moment gave a laugh and said, 'You've got me again. How d'you do it?'

He got up, laid a hand for a moment affectionately on Colin's shoulder, then came through the french window into the room.

Colonel Barrow said, 'Our neighbour, Mr Greer. Mrs Lawley.' To the man he added, 'Mrs Lawley has come to look after us till Dorothea is well enough to cope again. Sherry, Conrad?'

'Thank you.'

The man was the one of whom Constance had a faint recollection from the occasion when she had ventured into his shop to spend a little more than she could really afford on a small Chelsea bowl that had taken her fancy. She had often passed the shop and had paused to look at the bowl with steadily growing desire a number of times before finding herself turning almost without any intention of doing so into the shop and asking the price of it. It now stood on the mantelpiece in her sitting-room and she was as much in love with it as ever.

She remembered that there had been a woman in the shop as well as the man, but it was he who had attended to her and she could now remember nothing about the woman. The man was tall, dark-haired, dark-eyed, with thin, sharp features, wide shoulders and a lounging, loose-limbed way of moving which is possible only to the well-muscled. Today he was wearing tan trousers and a cream-coloured shirt which looked casual yet somehow costly. She thought that he was about forty-five or perhaps even fifty, but was someone who would always carry his years lightly.

'Good evening, Mrs Lawley,' he said. 'I'm so glad my friends have someone to look after them. Not that Colonel Barrow couldn't manage. He's an immensely practical man, you'll find. But I know if Mrs Barrow saw him busy with the dishwasher, for instance, she'd be itching to push him out of the way and do the job herself, even though she ought to be taking things very quietly.' He had a slow, gentle way of speaking in a deep voice that was softer than seemed to match the powerful look of his tall body. 'Haven't we met before, Mrs Lawley?'

'I came into your shop once,' she answered, surprised that he should remember her.

'Ah yes, some time ago, wasn't it?'

'I should think about two years.'

'As long as that?' He smiled. 'It just shows how few customers I have if I can remember for such a time the ones who come in and actually buy something instead of just asking if they may look around and going out again, empty-handed.'

'Conrad!' Colin called from the terrace. 'Come and play another game.' He had set the chessmen up again on the board. 'And don't throw the game away like you did last time. Come and play properly.'

'No, I must go home,' Conrad Greer answered. He sipped his sherry. To the Barrows he went on, 'I didn't throw the game away, you know. The boy's getting very good. I used sometimes to let him win on purpose, but not any longer.'

'He's so good at mathematics too,' Mrs Barrow said, and sighed as if this were something that faintly worried her. 'I suppose it's good to be clever at something, but of course he'll never be quite like other children. If only he enjoyed cricket or football or something.'

'I hated them both when I was his age,' Conrad Greer

said. 'I'm glad he's spared them at that school he goes to.'

Mrs Barrow explained to Constance, 'He goes to that special school in Bracklington for—well, for handicapped children. Handicapped—doesn't that sound awful? We did try sending him to the Academy, but he was miserable there. The other children realized he wasn't just ordinary and bullied him dreadfully. Yet he's so clever at some things.'

'Perhaps he'll turn out a great mathematician,' Conrad Greer said. 'Most mathematicians are slightly mad.'

'But he isn't *mad*!' she exclaimed in a horrified voice. 'You don't really mean that.'

'No, of course I don't—not in that sense,' he replied. 'I just meant a little inoffensively crazy.'

'You've always been so good to him. I don't think there's anyone he cares about as much as you.'

'Well, he's a lovable boy in his odd way, and one can see life's going to be hard for him.'

'What I should like,' Colonel Barrow said, 'is to keep him at home and have a tutor for him, but we couldn't possibly afford that. So it's a choice between the special school where he doesn't really belong or a common-or-garden public school where he'd be miserable. Of those two I prefer the special school. In another year, anyway, he can leave school and perhaps we can manage to get him some coaching which might get him into a university, if his maths are really as good as they say.'

'Or perhaps he'll do some growing up, given time. It's his birthday one day soon, isn't it?'

'On Sunday,' Mrs Barrow said. 'We've ordered a cake from Jennifer.'

Greer finished his sherry. He turned back to Constance.

'You won't have met Jennifer yet, Mrs Lawley,' he said, 'but I'm sure you will. She's something special. She runs a little café in the village where the cakes are home made and actually eatable and the coffee's excellent. A nice girl too.

You must ask Colonel Barrow to take you there to meet her.'

'Mrs Lawley made us a sponge cake for tea which was delicious,' Mrs Barrow said as if she were coming in a hurry to Constance's defence. 'Of course, Jennifer is a professional, but I can tell already we're very lucky to have got Mrs Lawley to come to us.'

'Of course you are.'

Greer stooped and kissed Mrs Barrow on the cheek, smiled at Constance and went out on to the terrace again, his usual way, she supposed, for getting to his home.

That last glance of his had taken Constance to some extent by surprise, for it seemed to her that for a moment his eyes, with a probing shrewdness in them, were assessing her with what was almost distrust. Perhaps it was not to his discredit that he should want to make sure that in fact the two old Barrows were really as fortunate as they had leapt to the conclusion that they were in having her to look after them, that she was not likely to extort money from them by devious means or make off with the silver. Yet there was something chilling about the brief look that he had given her, though when he had gone she quickly forgot about it. When she thought of him later she remembered only how kind he had seemed to be to that odd boy, Colin.

If she had been twenty years younger, she thought, she would probably have found the man very attractive. Being sixty, she saw this quality in him with what was really a very comfortable feeling of detachment. There was no challenge in it, no sense that she ought to be provoked into competition with anybody else. There were certain compensations, after all, in growing old.

Next day she had a talk about Colin with Mrs Newcome, the woman from the village who came in twice a week to clean the house. She was a tall, bony woman of about fifty with a long, lugubrious face and not much desire to gossip.

On arriving she immediately extracted the vacuum cleaner from its cupboard and went to work, recognizing Constance's presence in the kitchen only by a terse greeting and the observation that it wasn't as fine as it had been yesterday and that she wouldn't be surprised if there was rain before evening. She was dressed in trousers which fitted her gaunt figure admirably and a brightly spotted red and white shirt. Her thick grey hair was stylishly arranged as if she had just come from the hairdresser.

Presently, about half way through the morning, she sat down with Constance for a cup of coffee. Some time before that Constance had taken breakfast up to Mrs Barrow who had told her gratefully that breakfast in bed was one of the luxuries of life that she most enjoyed and had exclaimed at how good of Constance it was to have struggled upstairs with the tray. Colonel Barrow and Colin had had coffee and toast and marmalade in the sunshine on the terrace, then the Colonel had gone off to work in the garden and what Colin was doing Constance did not know.

She said to Mrs Newcome that it seemed to her that the Barrows were particularly nice people.

'That's right,' Mrs Newcome said. 'I've been working for them ever since they came here and that's twelve years ago or more, so I should know. They don't criticize, don't interfere with you, just let you get ahead with your work, and generous too. Give a good deal to things in the village, though they don't mix in much. I suppose they like a quiet life after all the travelling around the world they had to do, him being in the army and being posted from one place to another, India, Italy, Cyprus, Malaya, and then living in Bracklington for a time after he retired from the army and went into business of some sort there. Never had a real home of their own till they come here. It was for the sake of the boy they done that. Of course he was only a tot when they come, you couldn't tell how he'd turn out.'

'Then his parents were dead already?' Constance said.

'That's right. Killed in a car crash on one of those motorways. My husband won't drive on a motorway if he can help it. He's a decorator and works for a firm of builders in Bracklington, but he does a bit of gardening for people hereabouts when he's got some spare time. He looks after Mr Greer's garden for him. He's a neighbour of Mr and Mrs Barrow.'

'I met him yesterday evening,' Constance said. 'He runs an antique shop in Bracklington, doesn't he?' Remembering vaguely the woman whom she had seen in the shop on the occasion when she had gone into it, she asked, 'Is he married?'

'No, he lives alone. Well, I say alone. That's most of the time.' Mrs Newcome made a grimace which might have been taken for a rather lewd wink. 'He's a good-natured sort of man, I'll say that for him. Says he's sure the boy's going to turn out all right in the end.'

'He's a nice boy, isn't he?' Constance said. 'Perhaps he's just what I believe they call a late developer. He seems very friendly.'

'Ye-es,' Mrs Newcome said after a slight hesitation. 'Yes, he's all right most of the time. Can be as nice as can be when he feels like it. But you want to look out with him, he's got a terrible temper. I've seen him shriek and storm and break things. I'm always very careful with him.'

They were both startled by the sound of the kitchen door slamming. Beyond it they heard the sound of running feet. A moment before the door had stood open. Now it was closed.

'There,' Mrs Newcome said, 'you see what I mean. I believe he was standing there, listening to what I was saying. I'm a fool. For all I know that's pushed him into one of his horrible rages.'

CHAPTER 2

When Constance next saw Colin there was no sign that he was in a rage or had been in one. It seemed to her that he was a little more aloof than he had been before and that his brilliant eyes, instead of dwelling on her face, avoided looking directly at her, but that might have been imagination on her part because she was watching for indications that he was upset. If he was angry with anyone, it was with Mrs Newcome. Once she had left the house he came into the kitchen and offered to help Constance lay the table for lunch. As it had been yesterday, it was only bread and cheese and fruit and before it Colonel Barrow came out, as he had before, and insisted that Constance should join his wife and himself for sherry.

When the bread and cheese had been eaten and the table cleared and Mrs Barrow, saying apologetically that she could not understand why she got so tired when she had done absolutely nothing, had gone upstairs to lie down, he suggested that Constance might like to go to the shops in the village with him and see if there was anything that she would like to buy for the evening.

'We could walk, if you feel like it,' he said, 'or we can drive, if you'd sooner. I like the walk myself and it isn't far.'

'Let's walk,' Constance said. 'I'd like to get to know the village.'

'It's a pleasant place,' he said. 'We've lived here for some time now. We lived in Bracklington for a while after I retired from the army. I had a job as personnel director with Roberts and White's, but when Colin was left on our hands I gave it up and we moved out here because we thought it would be a better life for him. He likes you, incidentally. You can see that, can't you? It's lucky because between you and me he can be a little devil if he doesn't like a person. I don't know where he gets it from. His mother was a very quiet girl, almost too quiet, I sometimes used to think. Never cared much to play with other children and never wanted anything but to play the piano. Perhaps that was the trouble, I mean why Colin's not exactly—well, an ordinary boy. He may have inherited something from her. Her mother and I used often to worry about her.'

'What did her husband do?' Constance asked.

'Who? Oh, her husband. Oh well, he was in business. In Bracklington too, you know, that's where they met.'

That seemed to be all that he intended to tell Constance about his daughter's husband. As being 'in business' is one of the vaguest descriptions that can be given of anyone and as the Colonel's voice had become suddenly brusque when he replied to Constance's question, she deduced that he had had no great liking for his son-in-law. She wondered if he had been driving when the car in which he and his wife had lost their lives had crashed and if her parents blamed him for her death.

Presently the Colonel and Constance set off together for the shops. Mrs Newcome's prophecy that there would be rain before the evening looked as if it might come true. Clouds were beginning to pile up across the sky, blotting out some of the brightness of the sunshine, though in between them it shone brightly on the quiet countryside. The walk along the lane to the main road, then over the bridge and into the straggling village, took only about a quarter of an hour. Colonel Barrow walked briskly, holding himself as erect as ever and carrying a walking-stick in one hand and a shopping basket in the other. As they walked he started to ask Constance questions about her work, about the other people to whom she had been sent at different times and about her family. She spoke freely about her son, farming in New Zealand, but felt embarrassed at talking about her daughter. Could this kindly man understand a young woman who had chosen to live on unemployment pay in a community in the East End of London which indulged in vague good works in the inner cities, worshiped some strange god and for relaxation went in for a great deal of chanting? Constance could not understand it herself.

But the Colonel seemed to have a fair understanding of his grandson, so perhaps the girl's eccentricities would not seem too incomprehensible to him after all.

The first shop at which they stopped was a butcher's, where Constance chose a leg of lamb and some bones of which to make stock. Colonel Barrow did not pay for them, but had them put on his account. He told her that if she was shopping by herself during the next few days she need pay for nothing, as he had accounts everywhere. From the butcher they went on to a shop that was mainly a grocer's, but which also stocked fruit, vegetables, drink, cigarettes, newspapers, women's tights and a remarkable range of frozen food. It was a very modern, self-service shop and it would have been possible, Constance thought, looking round it, in spite of its being quite as small as village grocers used to be, to depend on it entirely for all one's needs.

She bought potatoes, a cauliflower and some raspberries and cream, all of which went into the Colonel's basket. She kept noticing other things that she would have liked to buy, but was afraid that the basket would become too heavy for him. They were just about to leave the shop when someone called out, 'Godfrey, darling!' and it appeared that Godfrey darling was the Colonel. He turned and smiled at a young woman who had just come up behind him.

She darted at him and kissed him on the cheek.

'You must come over and have a cup of coffee,' she said. 'You will, of course.'

'We've only just been drinking coffee at home,' he said.

'Well, have a little more. You must. I haven't seen you for ages.'

'Not since last week,' he said. 'Mrs Lawley, this is our

friend, Jennifer Hyland, the one we were telling you about
who makes the splendid cakes. Jenny, this is Mrs Lawley,
who's come to look after us till Dorothea gets better.'

The young woman smiled at Constance and said, 'Hallo.'
Then she asked, 'How is Dorothea?'

She looked about thirty and was short and somewhat
stocky, with curly fair hair cut short and brushed forward
over a low forehead, a broad face on which there was no
make-up, big grey eyes and a wide, good-humoured mouth.
She was wearing a sleeveless dress of dark green cotton and
bright red sandals on her bare feet.

'She's doing pretty well,' Colonel Barrow said. 'Why
don't you come up and see her?'

'I will, I will, as soon as I've a spare moment, I promise.
I've been busy making some things that have been ordered
as well as that cake for Colin. That's got to be a work of
art, of course. I'll bring it up myself and have a chat with
Dorothea then. Now do come across and have some coffee.'

'But if you're so busy . . .'

'Oh, never too busy for my friends. And I've got every-
thing I want here. I only popped across to buy some eggs.
I suddenly found I was running out of them.' She turned to
Constance. 'You'll come, won't you?'

Naturally, they went.

Jenny's Café, as it was called, was just across the road,
opposite to the grocer's. It was a thatched cottage with
beams in its white walls and at some time had had a very
inappropriate curved bay window let into its frontage beside
a door that stood open. Through the window Constance
saw small round tables covered with checked cloths and set
with cups and saucers.

Jennifer Hyland took them into the room with the bay
window where a few customers were having either late lunch
or an early tea, waited on by a brisk little woman in a
pink overall, and through the room to a garden behind
the cottage, where more small round tables under wide

umbrellas were dotted about a lawn. Setting Constance and the Colonel down at one of the tables, Jennifer said she would be back with the coffee in a moment and darted away. She did everything quickly, with a look of exuberant vigour.

'She's a dear girl,' Colonel Barrow said, 'and making a great success of this place, which I never thought she would when she started it. It's only been going for a couple of years. Conrad Greer found the cottage for her, just as he found our house for us. Her sister Julie works for him. Very interesting girl, Julie, but she and Colin don't hit it off, don't ask me why. Sometimes I think he may be a bit jealous of her, working for Conrad. Wasn't Dorothea saying yesterday that he worships Conrad and I don't think Colin likes him to care for anyone but himself. Absurd, of course, but that's what some children are like. They don't realize that other people have lives of their own.'

'Here we are, my dears.' Jennifer was back in the garden with cups of coffee on a tray. 'Now tell me all about yourselves, and tell me, do you want candles on Colin's cake?'

Her sister, Julie, Constance thought, must be the woman of whom she had a dim recollection in Conrad Greer's shop when she had bought her Chelsea bowl. There had been something very pleasant about that occasion, a feeling that the man congratulated her on having spotted one of the best things in the shop, even if a number of other things were more expensive. All that it had meant, of course, was that he was a very good salesman, but a sense that she would like to go back to the shop simply to meet him again had remained with her for a while. Then she had forgotten about him until she had met him the evening before.

'Candles, dear me, yes,' Colonel Barrow said. 'I'm sure Colin wouldn't feel it was the real thing without candles. And fifteen isn't so very many, is it? I mean, there'll be plenty of room for them. I can't remember when I stopped having candles on my birthday cakes. I suppose it was when I went into the army, because my birthday had a way of happening when I was in all sorts of Godforsaken places and I'd started thinking in terms of champagne, if that was possible, rather than cake. Then Dorothea and I started having birthday cakes again after we came here, but that was to amuse Colin. And we'd have just one candle standing in the middle of the cake and we'd let him blow it out and make a wish.'

'You've always been so wonderful with that boy,' Jennifer said, 'but I find it very difficult to remember he's fifteen. I know Conrad says in some ways he's very clever, but he seems such a child.'

A shadow of sadness passed across Colonel Barrow's face.

'Oh yes, and I suppose it's probable he'll never grow up. We've taken him to three psychiatrists, you know, and they all say he's got a very high IQ and he could catch up with other children quite easily if he wanted to. Only he just doesn't seem to want to. I know that's how it was with him with reading and writing. He simply wouldn't try to read until he was about seven and then all of a sudden there was nothing else he wanted to do and he could do it at once. We sometimes feel, you know, Dorothea and I, that it must be our fault. If he'd had a normal family life instead of coming to live with two such old people, we think he might not have clung so hard to being a baby.'

'Of course you've spoiled him terribly,' Jennifer said, reaching out and patting Colonel Barrow's hand with re-assuring friendliness. 'Terribly. But that's what grand-parents are for, isn't it? That's what our own were like to Julie and me. They let us get away with anything. We adored them.' She turned to Constance. 'Julie's my sister. She works in Conrad's shop.'

'So Colonel Barrow was telling me,' Constance replied.

'She really knows much more about antiques than he does. In the ordinary way she'd probably have been here this afternoon, because it's early closing in Bracklington, but she's gone to a sale in Oxford and I don't suppose she'll get home till the evening. She lives with me, but I don't see very much of her. She won't have anything much to do with the café. She thought I was mad to try to make a go of such a thing. But I thought she was mad to go into the antique trade. Sisters don't really know the first thing about one another, do they? Our parents wanted us both to be scientists or teachers or something like that and lavished education on us, first an awfully good, dreary sort of girls' school, then Julie went to Cambridge and I went to Edinburgh, and after all that she became a shop assistant and I took to cooking. Have you always done the sort of work you do now?'

'In a way, yes,' Constance said. 'That's to say, I've just lived a more or less domesticated life. But then when my husband died and both my children went away I felt I'd got to do something or I'd simply become a vegetable, and it happens that the sort of work I've been doing is the only kind I'm qualified to do.'

'What are your children doing?' Jennifer asked.

'Peter's joined a friend of his who's bought a farm in New Zealand,' Constance answered, 'and I think he's doing very well. And Irene—well, she's taken to a sort of social work.'

It was the best that she could do to describe Irene's peculiar activities without risking the embarrassment of having to explain what these were. The term social work fortunately was generally accepted as covering a multitude of strange goings-on.

'Does she live in Bracklington?' Jennifer asked.

'No, in London,' Constance said.

'But you live in Bracklington yourself, don't you?'

'Yes.'

'Then perhaps you know Conrad's antique shop.'

'I do, as a matter of fact.'

'The trouble is, he's such a snob about antiques, and Julie's got just like him. If you buy something you just happen to think is pretty and you pay what you think you can afford, they'll start pointing out to you that some repair work's been done on it and it isn't really all genuine, as you were told, and it's got a few worm holes or something and that you've paid twice too much for it. Since Julie's come to live with me I've stopped buying anything that isn't obviously and unashamedly modern, then she can't spoil it for me.'

The tone was cheerful, yet something gave Constance a feeling that the two sisters might have been wiser not to try to live together.

She said as much to Colonel Barrow when presently he and she started on their way back to Riverside.

'Have Julie and Jennifer been living together for long?' she asked. 'It sounds to me as if it might be a rather uneasy relationship.'

'Well, they are very different, that's true,' he said, 'but I'm sure they're very fond of one another. When we knew them first, we thought for sure Julie and Conrad were going to get married. That was some years ago, but nothing came of it. Whether or not there's been a—well, a relationship—' He broke off, giving a slight scowl which Constance thought was directed at himself. 'You see what it does to one, living in a place like Long Meldon. One turns into a terrible old gossip, there's so little else to talk about. It's worse than the army.'

'I think it's going to rain,' Constance said. 'Perhaps we ought to hurry.'

The sky had become quite overcast and a wind had started up which made the leaves of the chestnuts that lined the village street toss against one another.

'Yes,' Colonel Barrow said, 'yes, indeed. We mustn't have you getting wet and catching cold. We'd really be in trouble then, shouldn't we?'

Holding his walking-stick and the shopping-basket, he started to stride along faster.

But as Constance felt the first drops of rain on her face, a voice hailed them.

'Hallo, Godfrey! Hallo, Mrs Lawley!'

It was Conrad Greer.

Colonel Barrow said, 'What are you doing here at this time of day, Conrad? Oh, of course, it's early closing in Bracklington.'

'I was going to say, in another minute or two you'll be soaked,' Greer said. 'I've got my car here. Shall I drive you home?'

'Now that would be really kind,' the Colonel said.

'Wait a minute, then, I'll get it.' Greer strode off to where his car was parked.

In a minute or two he was back with it. The rain was already gathering force. Constance was glad that she would not have to walk through it all the way back to Riverside.

'How's Dorothea?' Greer asked as the three of them got into the car.

'Doing quite nicely, I think,' Colonel Barrow replied.

'In that case, I mean if you aren't in a hurry to get back to her, why not come home with me? I've something I'd like to show you.'

Colonel Barrow looked questioningly at Constance. 'We could do that, couldn't we?'

'Of course, if you want to,' she replied.

'All right, then—thank you, Conrad. Only don't offer us coffee, or tea either, for that matter. We had coffee at home, then some more with Jenny, and when we get home Dorothea will be wanting tea.'

'I won't even offer you a drink,' Conrad said, 'we English having been conditioned to think it's impossible to consume alcohol between three and half past five in the afternoon.'

'But surely it *is* impossible.' The Colonel looked troubled. 'Isn't it? Or is that really just this conditioning you're talking about?'

'Well, the French do it,' Greer said. 'I think even the Americans sometimes.'

'Is that so?' It seemed to be news to Colonel Barrow. 'Come to think of it, in India I used to have my whisky and soda at all sorts of odd times of the day. But that was because of the climate, of course. It upset all one's old habits. What do you want to show us, Conrad?'

'Wait and see. I'd like your opinion on it. I mean, if it's, well, suitable.'

'It's something for Colin's birthday, is it?'

'Yes.'

'You're always so good to him. I hope you haven't been too extravagant. I'm giving him a camera myself, not a grand one, just one of the kind you can get a print off straight away. I think he'll enjoy that more than having to wait while his film's developed.'

'I haven't got anything for him, but I'd like to give him something,' Constance said. 'Perhaps there'll be time for me to pop into Bracklington tomorrow and pick something up.'

'Oh, you mustn't bother,' Colonel Barrow said. 'He won't expect it.'

'But I'd like to. Birthdays are so important at his age.'

'Well, if you really would . . . Conrad, Jenny told us Julie's gone to a sale in Oxford today. Is she after anything special?'

'Yes, there's some good Spode in the sale. An unusually complete set, and of one of the rarer designs. But of course she'll keep her eyes open for anything else at all promising.'

'I wonder where you'd be without her.'

'So do I sometimes. Every time she picks up with a man I shake in my shoes. She'll get married some time, I suppose, and I'll have to look for a substitute, but I don't look forward to it.'

'Why not marry her yourself, then you can stop worrying?'

Greer laughed. 'If I haven't, you don't think it's for want of trying, do you?'

Colonel Barrow did not reply and Constance believed that that was precisely what he did think, though he would not dream of saying so.

The car had turned into the lane that led to Riverside, but on reaching it Greer drove straight past the gate and did not stop until they were about a quarter of a mile further on, outside a small, square house of dull red brick that had sash windows, a graceful fanlight above a white front door and a grey slate roof. Constance supposed it was Georgian. It had no front garden but faced directly on to the lane, and a wooden shed to one side of it was the only structure in sight that might be a garage.

Greer jumped out of the car and opened the door for Constance. Then he unlocked the white front door and gestured to her to enter quickly out of the rain, which by now was heavy. He did not trouble to lock the car. The Colonel reproved him for this, telling him that it was not fair to the police to be so casual.

Greer laughed again and said, 'Who's going to come along a lane like this and bother to steal a car as old as that? But I've got good locks on all my doors and windows and some alarm bells too, because it might get around that I sometimes have valuables here. Apart from that, do you know that more people are killed in their own homes than even on the roads? It's true that most people spend more time in their homes than anywhere else, so the statistics may not mean much . . .' He stopped abruptly.

He had just recalled, Constance thought, that the Colonel's daughter had been killed in a crash on a motor-way.

'Well, come in here,' Greer went on after a momentary pause, 'and tell me what you think of what I've got for Colin.'

He led them into a medium-sized room opening off the small hall. It had sash windows at either end of it, a small, elegant fireplace, a great many books and rather more furniture than it really needed for comfort. There was no sign of central heating having been installed and Constance remembered having been told that central heating was death to antiques. It might be a chilly place in winter, but if the rain had not been drumming on the windows now it would have been a bright and cheerful room.

'Here it is,' Greer said. 'I picked it up at a sale in Bracklington a week ago. Chinese, of course.'

What he was pointing to was a set of chessmen of red and white ivory, standing on a small table. They were taller than usual and the country of their origin was plainly to be seen in their finely carved Mongolian features. The knights were in elaborate armour, the kings and queens wore strange, lofty headgear.

'What do you think of it?' Greer asked.

Colonel Barrow did not look too sure. 'They're beautiful, of course, and if they aren't wasted on him . . . You know, he doesn't care for change. Of course he'll be delighted with them and he'll set them up and sit and gloat over them, but then he may put them away in a cupboard and go on playing with the old set.'

'Oh, he mustn't do that,' Greer said. 'These are meant to be played with.'

'But don't be disappointed if that's what he does.'

'Then tell him he shouldn't. Tell him I'll be very upset if he does. Tell him I won't come and play with him any more if he doesn't use them.'

'Yes, I can do that,' Colonel Barrow said, 'and perhaps it won't be necessary. I can never tell with Colin. I'm not clever with him, you know, like you. Perhaps he won't like my camera because he's set his heart on the most expensive thing on the market. He doesn't understand about money.'

'"It droppeth as the gentle rain from heaven upon the place beneath,"' Greer said.

'That's about it. But talking of rain, Conrad, are you going to drive us home?'

'Yes, of course.'

'These chessmen must have been horribly expensive. I do hope he'll appreciate them.'

'If he doesn't, he can give them back to me and I'll sell them. You're sure you wouldn't like some tea or coffee?'

'No, thank you.'

'Then come along.'

'But I'm sure he'll love them,' Constance said. She had stooped over the table to look more closely at the delicate carving of the chessmen. It worried her that Colonel Barrow should have been so discouraging to the other man. She could tell that he was hurt. 'Anyone would love them, even if they never played chess in their lives.'

'I know what Godfrey means,' Greer said. 'And it won't break my heart if they're a failure.'

The drive to Riverside took only a few minutes. As Greer drove off after leaving Constance and the Colonel and their shopping-basket at the door, he followed her into the house, then as she went to the kitchen, went into the drawing-room, saying, 'Dorothea?' But immediately he came out again.

'She's still lying down,' he said. 'I'll go and call her. You'll be getting tea, won't you? I don't know where Colin is.'

When Constance had made tea and put it with cups and saucers and the remains of her sponge on a tray and carried it into the drawing-room, she found that Mrs Barrow had come downstairs and was sitting in her usual place on the sofa beside the great fireplace, but there was no sign of the boy.

'I think he's in his room,' Mrs Barrow said. 'I heard him come upstairs. Perhaps he's fallen asleep. If you'd be so kind as to go up and see if he's there . . .' She looked up at Constance. 'He may be reading and not want to bother with tea. You see, when we're here by ourselves and haven't you to look after us, we don't usually have tea. I've a feeling, you know, that I haven't been looked after so well since I was a child. We always had tea then, of course, with hot buttered toast or crumpets, and cucumber sandwiches and a wonderful currant cake that our dear cook used to make.'

'What about India?' Constance said. 'Didn't you have a whole staff of servants there to look after you?'

Mrs Barrow looked a little embarrassed, probably at Constance having classed herself with a staff of servants when the old woman's instinct was to treat her simply as an unusually helpful guest. 'They didn't understand about crumpets.'

'I must see if I can buy some in the village tomorrow,' Constance said. 'And I'll go upstairs now and see if Colin is in his room.'

She found Colin in his bedroom, which was on the top floor of the house. He was lying on his bed, neither reading nor sleeping. His eyes were wide open, staring intently at some point on the ceiling above him. She thought that he was deep in some daydream and that he did not welcome being interrupted.

'In case you're interested, I've just taken in the tea,' she said.

He turned his head slowly on his pillow till his wide eyes, without having blinked, had become fixed on her face.

'Go away,' he said softly.

She did not answer, but withdrew, closing the door. But before she had reached the top of the stairs, the door had been flung open and he had come charging out.

'I didn't mean that!' he shouted at her.

'All right, then comb your hair and go down and have some tea,' she said.

'Yes, yes, of course I will, but I didn't mean to be rude to you.' He thrust his hands through his dark, curly hair, making it look even more unruly than it was already. 'I didn't think you'd really go away. Usually they don't.'

'Who don't?'

'Oh—people.'

She felt a faint chill up her spine. Did the boy see people who were not there? And if he did, what kind of people were they? Not that that was particularly important, it was only the question of whether or not they were there that mattered.

'There's still some sponge cake left,' she said, 'if you like it.'

'Oh, that's super. I'll be down in a minute.'

He shot back into his room and a moment after she had reached the bottom of the stairs, with his hair neatly combed, he came bounding down them and into the drawing-room, slamming the door behind him.

Constance went into the kitchen and began unpacking the shopping-basket that Colonel Barrow had left on the table there.

Presently he carried the tea-tray out to the kitchen. In spite of her insistence that she would do it, he stacked the cups and saucers in the dishwasher.

'You won't say anything to Colin about those chessmen, will you?' he said.

'Of course not,' she said. 'Birthday presents have to be a surprise.'

'What I mean is, I'm going to try to persuade Conrad not to give them to him. They're too valuable.'

'Won't Colin take care of them?'

'I expect so. Probably, but sometimes . . . The fact is, one can never be quite sure. Sometimes he can be very destructive and something as good as those chessmen is a responsibility. I realize that Conrad, being in the trade, may not have paid nearly as much for them as you or I would in a shop, all the same, he'd be very upset if Colin took it into his head to break their heads off. I remember a time—of course he was much younger then—when he had a teddy-bear he specially loved, and one day he got hold of one of my razor blades and cut it all to pieces. And there've been a few other incidents . . .' He closed the dishwasher

and turned to look at Constance with a slight frown. 'I
wouldn't say this to most people, but I've a feeling you
understand more than some would. D'you know, sometimes
that boy really frightens me. I don't believe he cares in the
least for his grandmother or me. I don't know what he does
care about. He seems to live in a private world that we're
all to keep out of. I think he cares more for Conrad than for
anyone, yet there are times when I get the feeling that he
hates even him. It's very strange.'

'It must be very difficult for you and Mrs Barrow,'
Constance said.

'Well, we've done our best and if things haven't worked
out quite as they should . . . Oh, I expect we worry too
much. If we've made mistakes we've always meant to do all
we could for the boy. Things may sort themselves out as he
gets older.'

He left the kitchen, but for once, as he went out, his
shoulders looked more stooped and his back less straight
than usual.

Constance started peeling potatoes to roast around the
leg of lamb, and turned on the oven.

It was about six o'clock and she had just put the joint
into the oven when the doorbell rang. She did not think that
answering the door was one of her duties and did not go to
it, but as she did not hear any footsteps crossing the hall
and as after a moment the bell rang again, she thought that
perhaps it was expected of her by the Barrows that she
would open the door and she went out to it.

She saw a woman standing on the doorstep with a suitcase
beside her, while a taxi was just disappearing out of the
gravelled forecourt. The rain was still falling steadily and
there was a cool, fresh scent of wet earth in the air.

The woman stared at her in a puzzled way and said,
'Who are you?'

She was about forty, slender, tall, dark-haired, with a
thin, tanned face in which her pale grey eyes looked

peculiarly vivid. She was wearing a raincoat with the collar
turned up around her thin neck and had a bulky bag slung
over one shoulder.

'I'm the help,' Constance said. 'Is it Mrs Barrow you
want?'

'The help?' the woman said. 'Do you mean you work
here?'

'For the moment,' Constance replied. 'Mrs Barrow's been
ill and I've come to look after things for her. Do you want
me to announce you?'

'That won't be necessary.' There was a curious twang in
the woman's voice that Constance could not identify. All at
once, picking up her suitcase, the woman pushed her way
past Constance into the hall. 'They know me. But I don't
know this house. It's new since my time.' Suddenly she
raised her voice. 'Hallo! Hallo! Is anybody there?'

The door of the drawing-room burst open and Colonel
Barrow came dashing out. For an instant he stood still,
staring incredulously at the woman, then he took a swift
step forward and clasped her in his arms.

'Margot!' he cried. 'Oh my God, Margot!'

She clung to him as tightly as he to her.

'Yes, it's Margot,' she said with a sob in her voice.
Constance saw the gleam of tears in her eyes. 'Oh, say
you're glad to see me. Say it, say it!'

'Yes, I'm glad, my darling, I'm so glad!' Then he half
turned away from her and shouted over his shoulder,
'Dorothea, it's Margot!'

Looking even paler than usual and unsteady on her feet,
Mrs Barrow appeared in the drawing-room doorway. She
held out her arms and the woman whom Constance had
just let into the house let go of the old man and went into
his wife's embrace. They kissed and clung to one another,
then Mrs Barrow took hold of the other woman by the
shoulders and held her a little away from her.

'This is so wonderful,' she said, 'but why didn't you tell

us you were coming? It's almost too much of a surprise. Is Kenneth with you?'

'No, I'm alone.'

'It's just a visit, is it, or—have you come to stay?'

'We can talk about that later. But I can stay now, can't I?'

'Of course, of course. Only . . .' Mrs Barrow glanced behind her. 'What are we going to tell Colin?'

'Why not the truth at last?'

'Is that what you really want?'

'Perhaps. I don't know. We'll talk about that later too. Where is my son?'

At that moment Colin appeared behind his grandmother. Constance thought that he had been there from the first when the mother and the daughter who had supposedly been dead for years had embraced, and that he had heard all that had been said. His big dark eyes which could look so fiery or so dull and empty were blazing as he stared at the strange woman.

'You're not my mother,' he said in a quiet, flat tone. 'I know you're not.'

'I am,' she said shakily. 'You're Colin . . .'

'You're not!' he suddenly shouted. 'You're not real, you're one of *them*, you're dead!'

He turned and vanished into the room behind him. There was a crash as of something on the terrace, perhaps the table with the chessmen on it, being overturned, then he must have fled into the garden, for there was silence in the room.

CHAPTER 3

Constance went into the kitchen and closed the door behind her. She ought to have done this sooner, she supposed, but uncontrolled curiosity had kept her where she was in the

hall. Reappearance from the dead is not an everyday occur-
rence. She had felt unable to move. But she could not be
welcome there. She had begun to divide the raspberries that
she had bought in the afternoon into three glass bowls that
she had found in a cupboard when she realized that they
would have to be divided into four. That was supposing
that the newcomer would be staying for dinner. She had
arrived with a suitcase, so it looked as if she intended to
stay.

If she did a room would have to be made ready for
her. Constance wondered if anyone would come out to the
kitchen with instructions for her or if she would be driven
into going into the drawing-room to ask what was to be
done. Meanwhile she laid the table in the dining-room for
four people.

As she went to and fro it across the hall she could hear
voices in the drawing-room, quiet voices, no longer excited,
but she did not hear Colin's. If he was still out in the garden
he must be soaked to the skin by now unless he had found
somewhere to hide. She thought of going out to look for him
herself and trying to persuade him to come in, but she was
afraid that if his grandparents had not already done this
themselves they might see it simply as an impertinent in-
trusion on her part. Opening the oven door, she basted the
leg of lamb and turned over the potatoes around it, then
put the cauliflower on the stove to cook.

She had just done this when Colonel Barrow came into
the kitchen.

'Please will you come and join us in the drawing-room
for a glass of sherry?' he said. 'We want you to meet
our daughter. And we apologize—well, perhaps I needn't
actually do that, you'll know what I mean. But we want to
explain this thing which I expect you think is really rather
extraordinary.'

'There's really no need, Colonel Barrow,' Constance said.

'Oh, there is,' he said. 'Of course there is. I mean, we've

lied to you about her, haven't we, and it must all seem very strange to you. And there's the problem of Colin. He'll expect you to know all about it and we've got to decide what to say to him.'

'Is he still outside?' she asked.

'Yes, but he's probably sheltering somewhere, in the toolshed perhaps. And I think we ought to have talked the whole thing over before we go looking for him. Come along now, and meet Margot. We've explained to her who you are and what you're doing here. We hadn't written to her about Dorothea's illness, so she was rather puzzled at first. We have been writing to one another occasionally during these past years, but naturally we didn't want to send her any worrying news.'

He opened the door into the drawing-room.

The first thing that Constance noticed was that she had been right, it had been the table with the chessmen on it that Colin had overturned on the terrace in his flight into the garden. The woman whom she had let into the house a little while ago was standing at the french window, gazing out, with her back to the room. She turned as Constance came in. The pale grey eyes that looked so vivid in her brown face rested on Constance with what she thought was hostility, but then the woman smiled and Constance realized that in a fine-boned, angular way she had remarkable beauty. She had taken off her raincoat and it and her shoulder-bag were lying on a chair. She was wearing a neat suit of a soft red with a deeper crimson blouse. She was holding a glass of sherry.

'Come in, Mrs Lawley,' Mrs Barrow said. She was sitting in her usual place on the sofa beside the fireplace. 'I'm afraid we've a lot of explaining to do, because we don't want you to think we're quite mad. Godfrey, give Mrs Lawley some sherry, and come and sit here, dear.' She patted the sofa beside her. 'Oh dear, I don't really know where to begin.'

'Begin with that slight slip-up of your daughter's,' the
woman by the window said as Constance sat down on the
sofa beside Mrs Barrow. 'I hope I shan't embarrass you,
Mrs Lawley, but I can put it in quite a few words and that
is how I prefer to do it. Colin is a son I had by mistake at
a time when I had a job in Bracklington just fifteen years
ago. But it happened that I didn't want to marry his father
and I did want to marry another man called Kenneth
Pauling. He's an architect and he'd just got a job with a big
firm of building contractors in Sydney. And he wanted
to marry me, but not plus a child. So when my parents offered to look after the child, Ken and I quietly vanished
away and we all thought it would be less upsetting for
Colin to believe we were dead than that we'd simply
abandoned him. We may have been wrong and of course
he'd have had to be told the truth sooner or later, as quite
a lot of people know I'm alive and one of them was sure to
tell him about it before he was much older. What none
of us knew, of course, was that he was going to turn
out a somewhat peculiar child, as I understand from my
parents he has. I can see it's going to be difficult to get
him to take in what happened. Anyway, now you know
the facts.'

'Would you like me to leave?' Constance asked.

She found something unnerving about the cool, hard tone
in which the woman had told her story. The faint twang in
her voice, Constance recognized, came from what she had
picked up of an Australian accent during her years in
Sydney.

Mrs Barrow put her hand quickly on top of one of
Constance's.

'Leave? Why should you think we want you to leave?'

'I only thought that with Mrs Pauling here to look after
you, you might not need me any more,' Constance replied.

'But do you want to go?' Mrs Barrow asked. 'Aren't you
comfortable here with us?'

'Of course I am,' Constance said.

'Don't think of moving on my account,' Margot Pauling said. 'I don't know what my plans are. If Colin can't stand the sight of me it might be best for me to move on soon. I may be moving anyway.'

'Don't say that now that you're back here after all this time,' Colonel Barrow said. 'You must at least take some time to think out what you really want to do.'

'You see, Mrs Lawley, I haven't actually told you all the facts yet,' the tall woman said. 'That marriage of mine, for which I gave up Colin and one or two other things, such as a man who I believe was fairly genuinely in love with me, has come unstuck. I needn't go into why, but there were good reasons and I walked out on it a couple of days ago, so here I am. But naturally I can't stay here indefinitely. I've got to earn a living and I can hardly do that in Long Meldon. I'll be moving on to London soon, I think.'

'Darling, you know you can stay here as long as you like,' Mrs Barrow said. 'Of course you won't stay for ever, but you can take your time and find yourself some really nice sort of job and just give us a little of the pleasure of your company after all this time.'

Constance did not feel that the company of Margot Pauling would give her a great deal of pleasure, but her parents of course would feel differently about it.

'I'll get a room ready for Mrs Pauling, shall I?' she said. 'Which room shall it be?'

'The one on the top floor, if you'd be so very kind,' Mrs Barrow said. 'The one next to Colin's. You know where the sheets and towels and everything are, don't you? Oh dear, I'm afraid this is more than you bargained for, but I do so hope you'll stay.'

'You see, she doesn't trust me to look after things properly,' Margot said, 'so I also hope you'll stay.'

Turning away, she gazed out into the garden again,

perhaps looking for where Colin might be hiding, or perhaps just looking at an English garden again after so long away from one.

Constance gulped her sherry and hurried out to the kitchen to inspect the roast in the oven.

She went to bed early that evening. Before she had served the dinner she had heard Colin's voice in the drawing-room and wondered what he was making of the situation, but had restrained an inclination to eavesdrop. But when she was in bed, finding it very difficult to keep her attention on the detective story that she had brought with her, she found her thoughts straying with a sad sort of curiosity to the boy, faced as he must feel himself to be by a fantastic problem.

In the morning she took Mrs Barrow's breakfast up to her in her bedroom, set the table in the dining-room for the Colonel, his daughter and his grandson, then settled down at the kitchen table to drink her own coffee. She thought that if she could think of a good reason for it, she would like to go home. Until the evening before she had been unusually happy in the household, very much preferring it to many others where she had worked, but the coming of Margot Pauling had already changed the atmosphere. Even if she made no difficulties of a practical nature, her mere presence seemed to have created a feeling that Constance was some-one to be kept at arm's length. She had often encountered this in other households, but not after such a warm welcome as she had received here.

She had cleared the dining-table, made the beds, cleaned the bath, done a little dusting and returned to the kitchen when Colin came into it. Though Constance had encoun-tered Margot once or twice during the rudimentary house-work that she had been doing, she had had no offers of help from her. All that Margot had said was that she hoped that she was not in the way, then she had strolled out on to the terrace where the table and the chessmen had been righted, had dropped into a chair and had lighted a cigarette.

Seeing this, Constance had reflected that she must find something that could be used as an ashtray, because there was no such thing in any of the Barrows' rooms. She was looking at the china and glass in a cupboard in the kitchen for some dish or bowl that would do when Colin came in.

He stood watching her for a moment without saying anything, then asked, 'What are you doing?'

'Looking for an ashtray,' she answered. 'Look, what do you think of this?' She held out a pretty little Davenport dish that she had just found in the cupboard.

'Why d'you want an ashtray?' he asked. 'No one here smokes.'

'Your mother does. She's almost a chain-smoker.'

'I wish you wouldn't call her my mother,' he said. 'My mother's dead.'

She gave him an uncertain look, wondering what he really thought.

'She isn't *my* mother,' he said as if he were explaining something very simple which she should have understood without needing the explanation.

'The mother you've always dreamed of?' she asked. 'She isn't like that?'

He sat down at the table, put his elbows on it and took his head in his hands.

'Do you like me?' he asked abruptly.

She was taken aback by it, but answered calmly, 'Of course I do.'

'Don't say that!' he responded in a soft, violent tone. 'Everyone says of course this and of course that and it doesn't mean anything. Everyone pretends to like me and says of course they do, but nobody does.'

'Oh, you're wrong, Colin' she said. 'Think how your grandparents love you.'

He gave a mocking little smile which reminded her suddenly of his mother.

'They've lied and lied to me,' he said. 'All my life they've lied to me. Do you lie to someone you love?'

She felt very helpless. 'Sometimes more, I think, than to anyone else.'

'No, you don't. If you do, it's because you don't trust them. That's just as bad as not loving them. Nobody's ever trusted me.'

She supposed that in a sense he was right, but she said, 'Of course they have.'

'Of course, of course!' He brought his hands down with a bang on the table. 'I wish you'd be serious. I thought you would be. You know what it's like here, you know I'm not wanted. This woman you call my mother didn't want me and Grandma and Grandpa only look after me because if they didn't people would talk. You don't know how often I've thought of running away.'

'Where would you go to if you did?'

'How do I know? That would be the whole point of it— not knowing where I was going.'

'What would you do for money?'

'Get odd jobs.'

'Now it's you who aren't being serious,' Constance said, but she was careful to keep her tone quiet to match his, as if they were having a reasonable discussion. 'It isn't as easy as all that to get odd jobs.'

'I'd manage. Or there are other things I could do. I've often thought about it and now that this woman's come here I'll have to do something.'

'What kind of thing?'

He gave her an odd look that was almost sly.

'Oh, I'll think of something.'

'Colin, dear, you know that sooner or later you'll have to face the fact that she really is your mother.' She did not know if this was the right sort of thing to say to him, or if it would be wiser to keep silence. 'She has her own difficulties, you know, and when she left you with your grandparents she really thought she was doing the best she could for you.'

'Do you love your own children?' he asked.

Again she was taken by surprise. 'Very much.' But as she said it she suddenly wondered how true it was that she still loved Irene and thought that it was strange that she had never asked herself this question before.

'Do you love them so much you'd die for them?' Colin asked. His tone was still quiet, yet there was extreme intensity in it and his eyes were blazing in his beautiful face. 'Do you?'

'I suppose it would depend on the circumstances,' she said, hoping that she did not betray how disturbing she found the question.

'Nobody's ever loved me enough for that,' he said.

'Do you want someone to die for you, then? I don't think it's a very nice thing to want.'

'You might like to know if they'd do it if you'd never been loved yourself.'

'But you have been. I told you, your grandparents love you very much indeed.'

He gave a little shake of his head. 'And I told you, they've lied to me all my life. As they'd have gone on lying if that woman hadn't come here. And even now they're lying to me about my father. They won't talk about him. They won't tell me anything about him. And my mother says he was killed in a car crash and that the only lie I've been told is that she was with him. She said it was because he was dead that she married another man and went to Australia. That's so silly.'

Constance was inclined to think that it was very silly, but that the real silliness for which the old people and their daughter were sure to pay now was that the boy had not known the truth from the beginning. All the same, she wondered if the Barrows knew who his father was and what had happened to him. In Margot's very frank statement to

Constance the evening before it was the one thing that she had not mentioned.

Colin sat in silence for a moment, then with the suddenness of most of his movements, he got up and left the kitchen. Constance sat down at the table and like him put her elbows on it and took her head in her hands. She felt that she had hopelessly mishandled the interview that she had had with the boy, yet did not know what line she might have taken with him that would have saved him from some of the intense unhappiness that he was experiencing now. And brooding about it did not help. After a little while she turned her attention to what she would give the family for lunch.

The simplest thing would be to give them some cold lamb left over from the evening before and some salad and then biscuits and cheese. But she had the evening to think about and that meant that she must go shopping in the afternoon. She could go to the butcher to whom Colonel Barrow had introduced her the day before; alternatively she might drive into Bracklington and go to the shops she was used to and while she was at it, pick up something as a birthday present for Colin.

This was what in the end she decided to do. When she had eaten her own lunch in the kitchen and cleared the table in the dining-room and Mrs Barrow had gone upstairs for her afternoon rest, Constance told Colonel Barrow what she was going to do and that she would not be away for very long, then got her Mini out of the garage and drove off. To be by herself without the pressure of other people's problems felt very peaceful. The day was sunny and warm and she enjoyed the drive to her home where she had thought that she might drop in for a few minutes to see that all was well and if there were any letters for her.

Meanwhile, she had to decide what to buy for Colin. It would have been so much easier if he had been a girl. She could have bought her a pretty scarf or some little trinket. And if he had been a few years younger she could have

bought him a toy, and if he had been a little older, perhaps
a book. But a boy of fifteen of whom she really knew very
little was a problem. There must be books that would
interest him, but she did not know what they were. In the
end, feeling that it was a confession of failure, she decided
on a book token. Perhaps it would give him pleasure to go
and choose something for himself. Stopping at a bookshop
near her home, she went in and bought the token, then
drove on to her house.

There were no letters except an electricity bill and an
envelope asking for Christian Aid. Putting them on her
writing-table so that she would not forget to deal with them
when she came back to stay, she went quickly round the
house and saw that all was well. There had been no break-in,
no tank had overflowed. It was a small house in a Victorian
terrace with only four rooms but all of them lofty and of
reasonable size. She had moved into it after her husband's
death, when Peter and Irene had both left home and the
house where she had lived for twenty-five years had started
to feel depressingly big and empty. She stayed in the little
house now for about ten minutes and was about to leave
when something stopped her. Going to her writing-table,
she sat down at it and began to write a letter to Irene.

It was a thing that she very seldom did. She did not
believe that letters from her were particularly welcome. But
something about the talk that she had had with Colin made
her feel that if her daughter should want to be free of her,
it ought not to be because of any rejection by herself. It was
a short letter, telling Irene where she was working and a
little about the problems that seemed to be developing there,
saying it would be nice to see her sometime and asking her
if she was happy and well. Leaving the house, she dropped
the letter into a post-box near it, then went on to the
supermarket where she did most of her shopping, bought
some veal escalopes and some fillet steaks, some fruit and
some vegetables, and set off for Long Meldon.

She arrived at Riverside in time to take tea into the drawing-room and found Margot Pauling sitting there by herself. She was wearing blue slacks and a blue and white striped shirt and would have looked coolly handsome if there had not been something ravaged about her face, healthy though it looked, tanned by the Australian sun. She seemed to make an effort to be courteous to Constance.

'Isn't it strange, I feel far more exhausted today than I did yesterday?' she said. 'It's trying to get used to the difference in time, I suppose. You're about ten hours behind us. And the journey itself took about twenty-five hours and I can never sleep on an aeroplane. I know I could have broken the journey at Singapore, but once I'd made up my mind to come home I wanted to get here as fast as possible. When I'm feeling a bit more normal I'll give you some help.'

'It's all right, I can manage,' Constance said. 'It's my job, after all.'

'I've got to look for a job,' Margot said. 'I've been running an interior decorator's in Sydney, and perhaps I could get into something of the same sort here, but I dare say there aren't so many opportunities going. I trained as a nurse once, years ago, but I'd be hopelessly out of date now. And I was never meant for that sort of work anyhow. Sick people —well, of course I know what's the matter with me, I'm thoroughly selfish. Sick people rather bore me, that's the truth.'

Constance could not resist saying, 'And children too?'

Margot gave a cold little smile. 'You're thinking of Colin? That child hates me, can't you see that? He doesn't want me to take him over. And anyway, how would I look after him if I was working? He's much better off with Ma and Pa than he would be with me.'

'You may be right.' It was Constance's formula for the times when she did not want to be drawn into an argument.

'Certainly I'm right,' Margot said with a curious bitterness in her voice as if after all she was hurt by her own conclusion. Yet probably she was right, Constance thought, and feeling a little guiltily glad that the problem of the boy and his future was not one to which she had to find a solution, went out to the kitchen and to the cup of tea that she had left there for herself.

At about six o'clock Colonel Barrow, as was his custom, came out to the kitchen to invite her to join the family in the drawing-room for sherry. She explained that what she was cooking for dinner would need her attention, but he persuaded her to go with him for a very quick drink. Mrs Barrow had come downstairs and she and Margot were sitting side by side on the sofa, Margot with a cigarette in her mouth, while Colin was on the terrace, poring over his chessboard. He glanced up as Constance came into the drawing-room, but his attention immediately returned with a look of deep absorption to his game against himself. It was only when Conrad Greer suddenly appeared on the terrace that he started up and exclaimed, 'Conrad! I say, that's super. Come and have a game.'

Sweeping all the chessmen over, he started setting them up for the beginning of a new game.

Greer said, 'All right, just one, in a moment.'

Then he came into the drawing-room to greet the Barrows and saw Margot.

He went rigid, staying where he was just inside the french window as if he could not move. But it was only for an instant. Then he came forward, smiling, and said, 'Well, well, Margot. What a surprise.'

She gave him one of her tight-lipped little smiles.

'You've a good memory for faces, Conrad,' she said.

'You haven't changed at all.'

'Oh, I've changed.'

'It doesn't show.'

'Because you've changed yourself,' she said. 'But one doesn't live as I've had to live without having it written on one's face, line by line.'

'Yes, the lines are there, I won't pretend they aren't, but they spell out much the same message as ever.'

'Conrad!' Colin was calling from the terrace. 'Conrad, come and play a game!'

Greer did not answer.

'Well, aren't you going to play with the boy?' Margot asked.

'Not just now,' he answered. 'Another time.'

'Conrad!' Colin cried. 'You said you would.'

'Yes, but I've just remembered something else I've got to do. I really haven't time to stay. I'm sorry, Colin.'

He stepped out on to the terrace and stood for a moment looking down at the boy, but it was as if he did not see him. Then he walked quickly away through the garden.

Constance wondered how it could have been that until that moment when the man and the boy had gazed at one another across the chessboard, she had never noticed what a remarkable resemblance there was between them.

She finished her drink and went out to the kitchen. She decided to cook the veal that she had bought in Bracklington. As she went to work, preparing it, she wondered if the Barrows knew that Conrad Greer was Colin's father. Once having seen the resemblance, she found it impossible to believe that they did not. But thinking over the brief scene in the drawing-room, it seemed to her possible that they had never realized it. They had shown no embarrassment when he had appeared, no evidence that they knew of any relationship between him and their daughter. The likeness between the boy and the man might have been something that had developed slowly and to which they were so accustomed that they had never noticed it.

Margot helped Constance that evening with clearing the dining-table and stacking the dishwasher and when this was done and Constance was thinking of leaving the kitchen and going up to her bedroom, Margot lingered, looking at Constance with an interest that she had not yet shown.

Constance was feeling unusually tired. It was possible, she thought, that she would soon have to give up the kind of work that she was doing and look for something less demanding. Meanwhile she wished that Margot would go, but, lighting a cigarette and sitting down at the table, she showed no inclination to do so.

'You live in Bracklington, don't you?' she said.

'Yes,' Constance answered.

'Why?'

The question seemed an odd one to Constance. 'Well, why not?' she said.

'But something must have brought you here in the first place, or were you born here?'

'No, I was born in London,' Constance said. 'But my husband was a lecturer in the Polytechnic here for twenty years.'

'And you never wanted to get away?'

'Why should I?'

'I'd have thought, if you've no ties, you might have looked for somewhere more interesting.'

'Nearly all my friends live here and at my age you don't make new friends easily.'

'Oh, you've friends here?'

'Well, naturally.'

'Is Conrad Greer a friend of yours?'

Constance understood now to where the conversation had been steered.

'I believe I've met him about three times,' she said. 'I don't think that amounts to friendship.'

'No.' Margot seemed to think this over carefully, then repeated. 'No. But you know if he still runs that antique shop, I expect.'

'Yes, I even bought something from him once.'

'And that woman Julie What's-her-name, does she still work for him?'

'I believe so.'

'Don't you know her?'

'No. I've met her sister who runs a café in Long Meldon, but I've never met Julie.'

'I used to think they'd marry, you know. I wonder why they haven't.'

It might be, Constance thought, that Margot herself was the reason. Alternatively, it might be that Colin was the problem. If Greer had acquired a wife and a home where between them they could look after the boy, Greer might have assumed that they should claim him and that perhaps might not have suited Julie. People can become as addicted to antiques as artists to painting, as composers to music, and giving up her work in the shop to look after a child who, so Constance had been told by Colonel Barrow, did not even like her, might not have appealed to her at all. Perhaps Colin had been right when he had said that no one had ever wanted him.

'Your parents know Mr Greer very well, I believe,' she said.

'They say he's always been very good to Colin,' Margot remarked.

'I believe he has.'

'Though Colin's not exactly a normal boy, is he? It may sound an absurd thing to say, but he rather frightens me. Those great eyes of his—'

She broke off as the front doorbell rang.

Constance was about to go to answer it when she heard the footsteps of the Colonel crossing the hall, so she pulled a chair out from the table and sat down, wishing that Margot would go, but she did not move. She only became curiously tense as she listened to her father's voice and that of the visitor and, drawing smoke deeply into her lungs, breathed it out again slowly through her nostrils. With astonishment Constance saw that the hand with which she held her cigarette was shaking.

The kitchen door opened.

'Margot,' Colonel Barrow said, 'it's your husband.'

She moved swiftly then, snatching at the handle of the back door, wrenching it open and disappearing into the garden.

Colonel Barrow came into the kitchen, followed by a tall man who looked about the same age as Margot though his hair was already grey. He had a square face with strong, stubborn-looking features, a wide mouth and light brown eyes spaced far apart under thick brown eyebrows. He was wearing grey slacks and a light quilted jacket and was carrying a small suitcase.

'That,' he observed, looking at the door that Margot had left open behind her, 'would seem to be that.'

Like her, he had picked up a faint trace of Australian in his accent.

'Mrs Lawley, this is our son-in-law, Kenneth Pauling,' Colonel Barrow said. 'I'm afraid we can't put you up here, Ken, all our spare rooms are occupied, but there's a very pleasant pub in the village that lets rooms. I'll ring them up and make sure they've got one free. Meanwhile come and meet Dorothea and have a drink.'

'Good evening, Mrs Lawley,' the stranger said. 'Perhaps I'd better go straight to the pub, Colonel. I wouldn't want to keep my wife out in your garden all the evening.'

'That's nonsense,' Colonel Barrow said. 'Seeing you suddenly like that, when she never dreamt you'd follow her, gave her a shock, that's all.'

'And what does she think I'm going to do to her now that I'm here?' Kenneth Pauling asked. 'Strangle the idiot woman?'

'I think it's just that this break-up of your marriage and coming back to England and all that sort of thing has upset her more than you'd think,' Colonel Barrow said. 'Her mother and I have both noticed that she's very nervous.'

'Who said that our marriage has broken up?' Kenneth Pauling asked.

'Well, she did.'

'I suppose she would. But we've a bit of talking to do before it's settled. You can't just pack a bag and write a note and prop it against a whisky bottle and get on a plane and think that's written off a dozen years of living together without a word of discussion.'

'Is that what she did?'

'Just about.'

'Anyway, she'll come in presently. So come and see Dorothea and have a drink and—and, of course, meet Colin.'

'Colin? That's the boy, isn't it? But I think, if you don't mind, Colonel, I'll go to that pub straight away, then come back tomorrow when Margot's got more used to the idea that I'm around. But of course I'd like to see Mrs Barrow first.'

'I'll ring up the Green Dragon at once,' Colonel Barrow said. 'I'm sure they'll have a room for you, but it's as well to be sure. Then I'll drive you down.'

'It's all right, I can walk,' Pauling said, 'if you'll tell me where the place is.'

'I could drive Mr Pauling to the Green Dragon,' Constance said, 'if you don't mind dinner being a little late.'

'Ah, that would be splendid, if you really don't mind.' The Colonel, she thought, would be glad to be free of his son-in-law and have a chance to discuss the situation as soon as possible with his daughter. 'Dorothea's been ill, you know, Ken. She's only just out of hospital. And Mrs Lawley's come here to help us. Now come along and I'll phone the pub.'

He led the man out of the kitchen.

It was not long before he returned and Constance took him out to the garage, drove her Mini out of it and waited for him to get into it. As he settled in the seat beside her she said, 'They'd a room for you all right at the Green Dragon, had they?'

'Luckily, yes,' he said. 'I'm not welcome here, am I? I didn't really think about that when I started off. I didn't know about Mrs Barrow having been ill and I didn't think Margot would run for her life when she saw me. It looks as if I've taken a long journey for nothing. Forgive me, but could you tell me who you are?'

Constance drove out into the lane.

'I'm housekeeper here for a week,' she said, 'till Mrs Barrow gets a bit better. I take on this kind of job from time to time.'

'They aren't specially friends of yours, then?' he asked.

'I never met them until Wednesday when I started work here.'

'So you didn't know Margot in the old days? I mean, before she came with me to Australia.'

'No.'

'I suppose they always thought I was wrong, leaving the boy on their hands.'

'Perhaps. I don't know. They're very fond of him.'

'What was really wrong with the idea I had then was that she and I could make a success of marriage after what had happened. Anyway, that's how it looks now. It isn't the first time she's left me, you know.'

'But it's the first time she's come all the way home, isn't it?'

'Yes.'

'And she always came back to you before?'

'When I fetched her back.'

'Perhaps she'll go back to you now if you really want her.'

'Oh, I want her. Damn the bloody woman, I've always loved her, though she's as neurotic as hell. Tell me, what's the boy like?'

Constance took so long to reply that after a little he said, 'Something wrong with him, is there?'

'I don't know quite what to say,' she answered. 'He isn't exactly normal.'

'You're saying he's crazy, are you?'

'Oh no, just that he's sort of strange. I think he's really quite a clever boy.'

'I get it,' he said. 'All my fault because of taking his mother away from him. That's what the psychiatrists say, isn't it? But that was her idea as much as mine, you know. I didn't care much one way or the other. Look, I don't know why I'm talking to you like this. I don't want to trouble you with my problems.'

'It's an odd thing, but doing the job I do I find people often want to unload their problems on me.' She was driving the car across the bridge into the main street of the village. 'I suppose it's because they're usually ill or under a strain of some sort and it's often easier to talk to a stranger than to someone you know well.'

'So I've been told, though I can't say I've ever experienced it before. Well, what about coming into the Green Dragon with me and having a drink? Perhaps you've some problems of your own you'd like to unload. I'm not as bad as you might think at listening.'

She thought that he might be very good at listening. In spite of looking big and tough there was a warmth and gentleness in his manner that made her wonder why Margot had left him. Infidelities, perhaps? A tendency to become quickly and easily involved with other women?

She answered, 'I'd like to, but I've got to get back now to get that dinner cooked as soon as possible.' She drew up at the entrance to the Green Dragon, which had once been a simple village pub but was now a quite sophisticated little hotel. It was a lop-sided looking building that had been painted a pale green and had a slate roof that sagged in a wavy line against the sky. 'I understand you'll be coming up to Riverside tomorrow.'

'D'you know, I'm not sure of that,' he said as he got

out of the car. 'I'll think about it. Thanks for the drive.'

As he spoke Constance saw another man walk up to the entrance to the pub and, catching sight of Pauling, suddenly pause.

It was Conrad Greer.

For a moment the two of them stood looking at one another in startled rigidity, then with an air of cautious formality, they shook hands.

Constance decided that it was time for her drive away, and turning, drove back the way that she had come. She had no sooner put the Mini back in the garage and gone into the kitchen by the back door, which as usual was unlocked, than Colin came running out to meet her.

'Where is he, what have you done with him?' he cried, catching hold of her by the arms and starting to shake her. 'That's the man who stole my mother, isn't it? He's why everybody's always lied to me. All my life, nothing but lies. I'm going to kill him. I'm going to kill everybody. That's what I'll do—'

Giving an eerie wail, he turned and dashed for the staircase up to his room.

CHAPTER 4

Colin appeared to have recovered somewhat by the time Constance announced to the family that dinner was ready, for though she did not see him again that evening she found, when she cleared the table, that someone had sat and eaten at his place. Colonel Barrow and Margot had cleared the table between the courses, so Constance had not had to go into the dining-room until the meal was over and Colin had disappeared by then. When she took coffee into the drawing-room he was not there. She went upstairs as soon as she could, got into bed and resumed reading her detective story.

But she soon laid it down as she tried to think how she would feed the family over the weekend. She would have to go shopping again in the morning. This was unlike her. Usually when she took on a job of the kind that she was doing here she immediately planned everything in advance, reduced shopping trips to a minimum, knew exactly what she would cook next day and felt that she had everything under control. But here things did not feel under control.

She felt that anything might happen to upset any planning that she might do. The front doorbell might ring again and heaven knew who might appear then. The two men whom she had left together at the Green Dragon perhaps, arriving together to make some fantastic scene about the woman whom they had once shared, or the child who belonged to neither of them. What kind of scene it might be she could not imagine, any more than she could guess what had happened after she had driven away from the pub. Perhaps it had all been very friendly. Perhaps they had even been glad to meet again after all these years. But if that doorbell rang again, she was not going to answer it. She had come here as a housekeeper, not as a marriage counsellor. And she was very tired.

After a little while she laid her book aside, turned out the light and soon fell asleep.

Next morning, when she had cleared away the breakfast, she sat down at the kitchen table to make out a shopping list. As next day was Sunday, some sirloin, she thought, would be appropriate. And that meant that the day after the family could eat cold beef. Then perhaps a gooseberry pie with cream might follow the sirloin. The list grew long as she thought of all the things which it might be useful to buy, but at last at about half past ten she got into the Mini and set off for the village.

It was as she was coming out of the butcher's that she met Kenneth Pauling. He had been buying a newspaper at the grocer's. He greeted Constance pleasantly.

'You wouldn't have a drink with me yesterday evening,'
he said, 'but what about some coffee now? I'm told they
give you a very good cup of coffee at this place called
Jenny's.'

'I haven't got long,' Constance said. 'I've a busy morning
ahead of me.'

'But you'll come—good.' He took the basket that she
held and carried it for her towards Jenny's Café. 'How do
you like it at the Barrows'?'

She did not answer at once because just then a car came
out from the garage beside the café and she saw that Jennifer
Hyland was driving it. Jennifer saw her and smiled and
waved, then drove off down the village street towards the
bridge.

'You asked me something,' Constance said. 'Oh yes, how
do I like it at the Barrows'? Very much, on the whole.'

They went into the café together.

'Not altogether, then?' he said as they sat down at a table
in the curved bay window.

'That would be rather much to hope for, wouldn't it?'
Looking at his strong, square face it struck Constance that
he looked as if he had not slept much. There were shadows
under his light brown eyes and deeper lines about his mouth
than she remembered seeing there before. 'When I take
these jobs I don't take for granted they're going to be easy.'

'What's difficult here?' he asked.

'A tendency unexpected strangers have of turning up,'
she said. 'The emotional atmosphere is getting rather highly
charged.'

'In other words, you're telling me I shouldn't have come.'

'Oh no, I'm not telling you anything, though you want
me to, don't you? Why don't you just ask me what you want
to know?'

They had given their order for coffee to a tall, slim woman
who it seemed to Constance she had met before. Yet she
did not think that she could have done so. Where could they

have met? The woman was in her late thirties, with fair hair drawn straight back from a somewhat stern-looking, handsome face and a casual air of waiting on them as if they were of no account to her. It was as she walked away that Constance suddenly realized why she felt there was something familiar about her. In spite of being tall and slender instead of short and stocky, and having sleek straight hair instead of a mop of curls, she had a distinct resemblance to Jennifer, whom Constance had just seen leaving the café. So this must be her sister Julie, who no doubt was helping out in the café because on a Saturday the antique shop in Bracklington was closed. And if Constance was right that this was Julie Hyland, she had certainly met her briefly before. She had been in the background in the shop when Constance had gone in to buy her Chelsea bowl.

Spooning sugar into his coffee, Pauling said, 'I'd like to know how long Margot stayed out in the garden last night.'

'I don't know,' Constance answered. 'She'd come in by the time I got back.'

'Because she knew I wasn't there any longer.'

'I suppose so.'

'Has she ever talked about me?'

'Not to me. She told me that Colin wasn't your child and that you'd only marry her if she left him behind when you went off to Australia. But yesterday evening you told me that was her idea as much as yours.'

He nodded, but his gaze had become abstracted.

'I did that, did I?' he said. 'Perhaps it's true. I always wanted to think so. I didn't like the feeling of having ditched the kid. I wanted her to be at least as responsible as I was. But it may have been one of the things that have always been wrong between us. Perhaps she was hankering after him.'

'I haven't seen any sign of that in her since she got here. She hasn't made any effort to get on good terms with him. To be honest, I don't think she likes him.'

'Is that because he isn't quite normal?'

'How do you know about that? Oh, of course, I told you that myself, didn't I? And you've been talking to Mr Greer.'

'Who's Colin's father. You know that, don't you?'

'I guessed it.'

'The way things happened, I ought to have realized then that it would be useless for Margot and me to go ahead with our marriage. We were engaged, you know, and I had to go away to work on a job in Scotland and when I got home from it she was pregnant. And that's how it's gone on, except that she's been more careful that there shouldn't be any more Colins. She didn't want us to have a child. I wasn't keen on the idea myself, so that didn't matter, but the devil of it is I'm fairly violent by nature and I've beaten her up more than once. Somehow we've always managed to forgive one another, but this last time we both went rather far and I think she got frightened. I know I did. I hadn't realized before just how much of the brute there is stored up in me. It's not a nice discovery. And when she ran out on me all I could think of was that I'd got to follow her and persuade her that it would never happen again and get her to come back. But you saw how she bolted the moment she saw me.'

'You called her an idiot woman then, as if it were absurd for her to be afraid of you,' Constance said. 'But that isn't quite what you're saying now. Perhaps it wasn't absurd.'

He sighed. 'No, I'm very mixed up. I was embarrassed yesterday evening because you and the old man were there to see what happened when Margot and I met. And I think, until that did happen, I hadn't taken the situation as seriously as I should. Perhaps what I was really thinking of was what an idiot she'd been to think she could go on getting away with her infidelities without pushing me beyond what I could take. I had an idea that if I followed her here it might be enough of a shock for her to make her realize we'd got to do a lot of talking before we called everything off and that perhaps both of us could change and make a reasonable success of things after all.'

'What I really don't understand,' Constance said, 'is why you're telling me all this. What is it you really want from me?'

'A spot of sympathy, perhaps.'

She shook her head. 'I think there's more to it than that.'

'All right then, I've been wondering if you could persuade her to come and talk to me here. I don't want to go back to the house. I'm not exactly welcome there, would you say? I think Margot may have given the old people a version of what's gone on between us which has rather suppressed the provocation I've had. And to tell you the truth, I don't want to run into that boy. He can't much want to meet me either.'

'I'm sure you're right there.'

'Well, will you ask Margot to come and meet me in the Green Dragon?'

'Yes, I can do that. And if she doesn't come, I promise it won't be because I haven't delivered your message.'

'I understand that. You might add, when you give it to her, that in the bar of the Green Dragon nothing very dangerous to her can happen.'

'What puzzles me,' Constance said, 'is why you want to stick together. I couldn't endure a relationship of the kind you've described.'

He gave a tight little grin. 'It rather puzzles me myself, but there it is.'

'You don't really think you're going to get anywhere with her, do you?'

He did not answer, but finished his coffee. Constance had already finished hers. The brisk little woman in the pink overall whom Constance had seen when she and Colonel Barrow had come into the café with Jennifer came to their table and tried to persuade them to have another cup. When they both refused she presented the bill.

'Where are you going now? Pauling asked as he and Constance went out into the street.

'I've some more shopping to do,' she said, 'then I must get back to Riverside and get on with my job.'

'And you'll give Margot that message of mine as soon as you can?'

'Yes,' she assured him.

As if it had only just occurred to him to answer her last question, he said, 'Of course it won't do any good, but we've got to talk things over. Money, for instance. Our home in Sydney, what's going to happen to it? Do we go ahead with a divorce? We've got to talk. She can have money if she wants it. Tell her that, though it may not help to persuade her to come. Goodbye for now. Thanks for listening to me.'

He turned towards the Green Dragon while Constance crossed the street to the grocer's.

She spent longer than she had intended in the shop. Her nerves were on edge after the talk in the café. She could not decide whether she liked or disliked Kenneth Pauling, and whether she was sorry for him or thought him dreadful. Thinking of her own marriage, which had been tender and faithful, marred only by the briefest of quarrels, yet which had had passion in it too, she told herself that however long she lived, she would never understand other people. She wandered slowly round the shop, filling the wire basket provided for the purpose from the shelves with far more things than were on the list that she had made before setting out, and found this soothing. After a while she began to feel that there was even a rather gruesome kind of comedy in the situation in which she found herself.

She had come to Long Meldon to act as housekeeper to an elderly couple, retired army people, kindly, conventional, considerate, the only strangeness in the household at first being their somewhat maladjusted grandson. They loved him, however, and he appeared in his way a sufficiently likeable boy. But then there had appeared on the scene a

distinctly maladjusted daughter, followed by a maladjusted
husband, while in the background there lurked the daughter's abandoned lover, father of the child and devoted to
him. And these people were showing signs of turning to
Constance for help. To Constance, who had had so few
problems in her life. It really was rather funny.

It was true that she had had her problems with Irene.
Those at times had seemed of immense importance to her.
Other people, she had thought, did not have such peculiar
daughters, and it had bewildered her that two such normal
people as she believed her husband and herself to have been
should have produced such a freak. But in Long Meldon, it
seemed, freaks were thick on the ground and it was just her
fate that she was stuck in the midst of them. Until next
Wednesday. That was really not so far away. She could put
up with it somehow. Heading for her car with all her
purchases, she got into it and started the drive back to
Riverside.

Driving the car into the garage, she entered the house by
the back door, which as usual was unlocked. She saw at
once that Jennifer Hyland had been here before her, for in
the middle of the kitchen table there was a large birthday
cake. It was a very fine cake covered with white icing with
elaborate pink decorations and with the words 'Many happy
returns, Colin' inscribed on its top.

Constance stood looking at the cake, considering it. It
could not stay where it was because she would soon be
needing the table to work at, and besides, there was the
question of whether or not Colin was to see the cake before
his birthday tomorrow, or whether it was to be kept a secret.
She decided to ask Mrs Barrow and, putting down the full
basket that she had brought with her into the kitchen, she
went to the drawing-room.

She started to scream.

She screamed and screamed.

*

It was a moment before she realized that it was she who was screaming. She heard the sound of it and she felt a constriction in her throat, but some time passed, she never remembered how long, before she connected the two things. When that happened she became abruptly silent and stumbling out of the room, went to the telephone in the hall. She dialled 999.

'Police,' she said. 'Please, at once . . . My name? Oh, it's Lawley . . . The address? Riverside, Long Meldon . . . I've just found four bodies in a room here . . . Yes, *four* . . . Yes, I said *four*, and I want the police at once.'

She seemed to have to wait for a never-ending time, yet at the same time she knew that it was almost at once that a man's voice said, 'Police. Bracklington. Yes?'

'Please send someone here at once,' she said. 'Riverside, Long Meldon. I've only just got in and I found . . .' She began to feel that she might be sick before she could say any more, but she forced herself to control it. 'I found four people all dead in the drawing-room . . . Do I know who they are? Yes, they're Colonel and Mrs Barrow and their daughter, Mrs Pauling, and her son. I think they've all been shot. There's a pistol, or a revolver or something like that, lying on the floor . . . Yes, I'm quite sure they're all dead . . . No, I don't know when it happened, I've been out, I told you, and only just got in . . . I work here, that's why I found them. Please send someone at once.'

She was told that someone would be with her almost immediately. She put the telephone down and only then realized that she felt deathly cold all over. The cold seemed to have got into her bones and to be spreading from them through the rest of her body so that she shivered violently. There was a moment when the scene before her went completely black, then a light that was almost too lurid came back and she saw that she was standing with her hand still on the telephone and that the door into the room where she had seen unspeakable things was open. She shot into the kitchen and slammed the door shut behind her. She felt as if she were in some extreme kind of danger which came seeping towards her through the closed door from that other room and that it was going to engulf her and smother her.

Then she began to come to herself and sat down in a chair at the table, still feeling the chill in her blood, but recognizing it with the beginning of rationality as a symptom of shock and understanding that she could look at the door without seeing something terrible come through it. She was not in any danger unless it happened that a murderer was loose in the house and was going to come looking for her. But the murderer was in that room, as dead as his victims.

Her eyes suddenly fell on the birthday cake on the table before her. 'Many happy returns, Colin.' She felt tears gathering in her eyes and beginning to spill on to her cheeks. Folding her arms on the table, she hid her face in them, so that she need not go on looking at the cake.

When the police came she went to meet them at the front door with a rather creditable appearance of calm. A man of about forty, of medium height, with wide shoulders, an almost triangular face, wide at the temples, sharp at the chin, a high forehead from which the brown hair had begun to recede, and small, shrewd, bright blue eyes, introduced himself as Detective-Inspector Frayne.

She said, 'Come in.' Then she stood back and gestured at the door of the drawing-room. 'In there.'

She watched him as he went to the door, followed by a tall, powerful-looking young man who stood just behind him, looking over his shoulder into the room.

This man said, 'Christ!' then clapped a hand over his mouth as if, like her, he felt an impulse to be sick. But it seemed to be only momentary for he seemed collected enough as he followed the Inspector into the room.

Constance wished that they would close the door, but

realized that they were following the regulations concerning touching nothing. After a moment they both emerged from the room.

The Inspector said to her, 'Have you got any brandy?'

'I don't know,' she said. 'Perhaps. Do you want some?'

'No, but you do,' he said. 'Where do they keep it?'

'In the dining-room, I suppose. I don't know.' She pointed. 'In there.'

He took her by the arm and guided her into the dining-room and to a chair at the long mahogany table. Going to the tall old sideboard, he started opening its cupboards till he found what he was looking for, a bottle of brandy and some glasses. As she watched him doing it, Constance had a feeling that she had seen something like this happen before, then she realized that what he reminded her of as he seemed to make himself strangely at home in the house was of how she herself behaved when she went to take up a new post. She always had to learn where her employers kept their china and their cooking-pots, their sheets and towels, as well as what food they had in their refrigerator or freezer. She always had to go searching through the house, opening cupboard doors and drawers until she knew where she could put her hand on anything she wanted. She had never thought that a policeman might be in the habit of doing virtually the same.

Pouring out some brandy for her, he said, 'I'll be with you in a minute,' and went out.

She heard him speaking on the telephone in the hall. She supposed that he was giving instructions to someone in Bracklington. Soon, no doubt, more men would arrive with cameras and with chalk to outline where the bodies lay, and with equipment for the search for fingerprints, and a doctor, of course. And after all that, no doubt, the Press. The Press! She shuddered. Would she be able to avoid the Press or would she have to talk to them? As soon as news of what had happened in the house got out, they would be certain to descend on it. Massacres do not go unreported.

She swallowed some brandy and felt it conflict with her inward chill and quickly drank some more. It seemed to steady her and with a sigh as if of deep emotional exhaustion, she closed her eyes.

But as soon as she did that she saw again what she had seen in the room. Mrs Barrow had been sitting on the sofa by the fireplace and Colonel Barrow had been sitting beside her. Margot Pauling had been in a heap on the floor, just inside the french window. Colin had been lying on his back in the middle of the room. And they had all had blood on them. A terrible lot of blood which looked very red and wet, as if it had only just started to flow. Mrs Barrow's face was half-hidden in a stream of it that seemed to come from a hole in her forehead. The Colonel had a great blotch of blood covering his chest. Margot's wounds could not be seen because of the way that she had collapsed, covering them, but there was a mess of blood on the carpet near her head. And half of Colin's head seemed to have been blasted away. There had been a revolver close to his right hand.

Constance opened her eyes again as she heard the Detective-Inspector come back into the room. The big man with him was introduced to her as Detective-Sergeant Randall. She could hear that there was someone else in the house and was told by the Inspector that there was a constable out there, keeping an eye on things.

'If you're up to it,' he went on, 'there are a few things I'd like to ask you before the others get here. It'll save time later.'

'Go ahead,' she said.

'Well, first, who are you?'

She told him her name and her home address and explained what her position was in the house. The sergeant had taken a notebook out of a pocket and began to write in it.

'And this morning you went out?' the Inspector asked.
'Yes.'

'Why did you do that?'

'To do some shopping. When I'm on a job like this I take
over everything, shopping, cooking and so on. There's a
Mrs Newcome who comes in twice a week here to do the
basic cleaning, but I do everything else.'

'What time did you set out?'

'I think it was about half past ten.'

'And was everything normal then?'

'Normal? Yes—no—I suppose so. I don't know. It can't
have been, can it?'

'But did you notice anything unusual?'

'No, but I think that was my fault. I ought to have noticed
something. If I'd taken the boy seriously last night . . . It
was the boy who did it, wasn't it?'

'That's how it looks, but it's a bit too early to say anything
for sure. It looks as if he somehow got hold of a gun and
killed the other three and then himself. But we'd better not
commit ourselves yet. What happened last night that you
didn't take seriously.'

She sipped some brandy. 'Perhaps I'd better explain
about the household here, then you'll understand. Colonel
and Mrs Barrow have been living here for some years with
their grandson, Colin. And Colin was brought up to believe
that his parents had been killed in a car crash. But the truth
is that he was the illegitimate son of their daughter who—
who's in that room. The one by the window,' her voice
cracked as she said it. 'And she didn't want him and left
him with her parents and got married to a man called
Pauling who was going out to a job in Australia and she
stayed there without Colin knowing of her existence until
last Thursday when she suddenly walked in here. She'd
broken up with her husband and come back to England,
saying she was going to stay and look for a job. And her
coming like that and his discovery that she'd been alive all

these years was a terrible shock for Colin. And he wasn't altogether a normal boy at the best of times.'

'What was wrong with him?'

'I don't know how to put it exactly. I don't know much about that sort of thing. He wasn't exactly what you'd call handicapped, but he was undeveloped in some ways, yet clever in others, and very emotional, yet he didn't seem really able to care for anybody. He was obsessed with the belief that nobody wanted him.'

'Didn't the old people want him? Weren't they good to him?'

'They were very good to him.'

'Then why did he have that idea?'

'I think it was just the kind of boy he was. And when he discovered that his mother was alive and when he came face to face with her, he became sort of wild with fury that he'd been lied to all his life. And that seemed to be very important to him, that he'd been told so many lies.'

'Can't say I blame him,' the Inspector observed. 'I get told a good many lies in the course of my work and it doesn't improve my temper. What about the man Pauling? He's stayed in Australia, has he?'

'No, he followed his wife here. He's in Long Meldon.'

The sergeant again muttered, 'Christ!' Constance began to wonder if it was his only word.

'He's staying at the Green Dragon in the village,' she said. 'He arrived here yesterday evening, hoping, as I understand it, to persuade his wife to go back with him. And Colin saw him and discovered who he was and shouted at me that he'd stolen his mother and that he was going to kill him and was going to kill everyone else too. Then he dashed up to his room and I didn't see him again until—until just now. And I felt terribly sorry for him, but I never thought for a moment of taking him seriously. I mean, children so often make fearful threats, but they've forgotten them in a few minutes when they've calmed down. If I had, if I hadn't been so blind and ignorant about people like him, I ought to have been able to prevent this happening.'

Inspector Frayne gave her a long, thoughtful look, as if he had not made up his mind as to whether she was at least partly to blame for what had happened, or whether he should reassure her that she should not start blaming herself for what could not have been prevented by anyone.

'That gun,' he said, 'do you know anything about it?'

'No.'

'It might have been Colonel Barrow's. A war souvenir. There are a lot more of those around than there ought to be. I wonder if he had a licence for it.'

'I don't know. No one ever said anything about there being a gun in the house.'

'But if there was one, the boy might have known about it, I suppose.'

'Yes, I suppose so.'

'And might have known how to fire it?'

'Well, he was clever at some things.'

'We'll have to check up on it. Now you went into the village shopping at about half past ten. By car?'

'Yes.'

'So it didn't take you long to get there. And when you came back you discovered that slaughter in the other room and you phoned 999 straight away. I've a note of that. That was at about a quarter to twelve. So you'd spent more than an hour shopping. You did a good deal, did you?'

'No, it wasn't like that.' All at once she felt distrust of him, wondering what words he might be trying to put into her mouth, and why he might be doing it.

'What wasn't?' he asked.

'I met Mr Pauling outside the grocer's and he asked me to have coffee with him and we went into Jenny's Café— and that reminds me!' She stopped, startled at herself.

'Yes?'

'Colin's birthday cake! You see, it was his birthday

tomorrow, and Jennifer Hyland was making a birthday cake
for him. And as Mr Pauling and I were going to the café I
saw her drive off and she waved to me. She was coming in
this direction. And when I got back here I came in by the
back door because I knew it wouldn't be locked and I saw
the birthday cake on the kitchen table. So she came here
sometime during the morning. Whether it was before or
after the shooting I don't know, but somehow it seems to
me . . .' She paused.

'Yes?' he said again.

'I was just going to say, it seems to me it could have been
after, because what I'd have expected her to do would have
been to go to the front door and ring the bell and only if
nobody answered it go round to the back and let herself in
and leave the cake. And of course, if it was after the shooting,
no one could have answered. But I'm only guessing. I think
she knew the Barrows pretty well and perhaps she knew she
could get in at the back and left the cake there as a surprise
for them.'

'You said her name was—?'

'Jennifer Hyland. She runs Jenny's Café.'

'And you're sure she was here this morning?'

'She must have been.'

'Because of the cake. I think I'd like to look at this cake.'

Constance stood up and led the way to the kitchen. There
was something dreadful to her about the cake with its
cheerful message, 'Many happy returns, Colin.' But Inspector Frayne looked at it with considerable approval.

'Artistic job,' he said. 'A professional, this Miss Hyland?'

'Oh yes.'

'And it's certain she came up to deliver it this morning?'

'Well, it wasn't there when I left and I saw her setting
out from the café as Mr Pauling and I went into it, so I
suppose she must have come here.'

'I think we'd better talk to her.' He took hold of his
sharp-pointed chin and began tugging at it thoughtfully

while he went on gazing at the cake as if it could tell
him something. 'My guess is, you know, that the shooting
happened only just before you got here. You didn't hear
anything?'

'No.'

'The forensic chap may say something different. Oh—'
He broke off. 'Here they are.'

He left the kitchen and went to the front door and opened
it.

Several cars had drawn up in front of the house and a
number of men streamed in. Constance heard their footsteps
and their voices, some exclamations of shocked surprise, a
whistle or two and even an altogether inexplicable laugh.
Someone with very bad nerves, she thought. She did not
know what to do with herself, stay where she was, return to
the dining-room or even go upstairs to her bedroom. She
could have stayed where she was if it had not been for the
cake which seemed to be hideously mocking the tragedy
that had happened in the house.

In the end she returned to the dining-room, slipping as
unobtrusively as she could through the hall which was full
of large men who looked at her with an air of wondering curiosity, but did not speak to her, and once in the
dining-room, she closed the door and helped herself to more
brandy.

It was only when she had been sitting there for some minutes
that she noticed that there was a telephone in the room,
with a directory beside it. Some more minutes passed before
she suddenly got up and moving softly as if she were
afraid of being caught out in doing something that was
not allowable, she went to the telephone. Picking up the
directory, she turned its pages till she found the number of
Jenny's Café, Long Meldon. When she dialled the telephone
gave a tinkle and she thought it might bring someone to see
what she was doing and wondered if it would be considered

improper. The presence of police in the house gave her a
feeling of irrational guilt, although she had felt something
far worse than that before their arrival.

She heard the ringing tone on the telephone and after a
moment someone said, 'Jenny's Café. Can I help you?'

'Can I speak to Miss Hyland?' she said. 'Miss Jennifer
Hyland.'

'I'm sorry, she isn't in,' the voice replied. 'Can I take a
message for her?'

'When do you think she'll be back?'

'I'm afraid I don't know. Who is it speaking?'

'I'm Constance Lawley. I've been working at the Barrows'
house for the last few days.'

'I'm Julie Hyland, Jennifer's sister. She was going up to
Riverside this morning. Didn't she come?'

'Oh yes, she came. And I wanted to ask her . . . Well,
I'll leave it for the moment.'

'Is there something wrong with the cake?'

'Oh no, it looks perfect.'

'I'm sorry I can't tell you when she'll be back. I expected
her some time ago, but when she didn't come I thought
perhaps she'd stayed for a chat with Mrs Barrow. She does
that sometimes. She's very fond of the Barrows.'

'No, she didn't do that.'

'Then I don't know where she is. She must have met
some other friend and gone in to have a drink with her or
something. She knows I'm here to keep an eye on things.'

'Well, when she does come in, would you tell her . . .?'
But again it seemed impossible to leave any message for
Jennifer, though it might not have been so difficult to talk
to her directly. 'Just ask her to ring up here when she gets
in, will you? It's rather urgent.'

'Something's wrong, isn't it?' Julie Hyland said. 'You
sound upset. Is there anything I can do?'

'No, no, I can't explain. But please just ask her to ring
up.'

'Yes, I'll do that.'

Constance put the telephone down. A moment after she had done it the door opened and Inspector Frayne appeared in the doorway. His small, bright eyes studied her for a moment before he spoke.

'I listened to that little conversation of yours on the telephone out here in the hall,' he said. 'I heard it tinkle. Why was it you wanted to speak to Jennifer Hyland?'

'Wasn't it obvious?' she said. She went back to her chair and picked up her glass of brandy again. 'I wanted to ask her what happened when she came here, whether she spoke to anyone or saw anyone and just when she came here. I don't know if she was coming straight here when I saw her leaving the café, or if she had other deliveries to do first.'

'I think that's a job you'd better leave to us,' he said.

'But I can't help being curious.'

'I'll tell you anything we find out, anything relevant. It looks a fairly straightforward case, though that doesn't make it any less horrible. Going by what you've told me, I understand the boy wasn't normal in the first place, and he'd had a very severe emotional shock. And that filled him with rage, against all the people who he realized had lied to him all his life, specially the mother who'd abandoned him, and he wanted to kill them all. It may be, you know, that if you hadn't gone out shopping this morning, you might have been one of them. You might be one of the corpses in that room. I think you can count yourself lucky.'

'Will there be an inquest?'

'Of course.'

'And I suppose I'll have to give evidence.'

'It's probable.'

'What do you want me to do now?' she asked. 'Do you want me to stay here or can I go home?'

'You said you live in Bracklington, didn't you? I can't see why you shouldn't go home, though I'd be grateful if you'd stay here for the present. Anyway, till the evening.

We don't know what may come up. But I can understand it wouldn't be pleasant for you to spend the night here alone.'

'I don't believe I could face it.'

'Well, all right then, go home. But not just yet.'

'I don't think there's any more I can tell you.'

'You never know. And you say you're curious. Don't you want to hear what the Hyland girl has to say when she gets home? I'd be glad if you'd wait until—well, till they've finished in that room. They'll be removing the bodies presently. And we'll want an official statement from you, covering what you told me when I got here. I'm sorry, I don't want to make it difficult for you, but you're the only witness we've got at present.'

She nodded, giving a sigh. 'I know. And of course I want to help if I can. But unless Jennifer Hyland can tell you something more, I think you already know all there is to know about the whole thing. You'll tell me when I can go?'

'Yes.'

He went out, closing the door behind him.

Constance stayed where she was, hearing the voices and the footsteps in the hall, yet feeling herself enclosed in silence in the empty dining-room. She did not think of looking at her watch to see what time it was or to keep any check on how long she sat there. Time seemed to pass very slowly until sometime in the afternoon when it suddenly struck her with a good deal of surprise that she was very hungry. The thought of eating was nauseating, yet her body was asking for food. She pondered which would be worse, to endure that need or to plunge out of the room among the men who were still busy at their job outside it and to make for the kitchen. Perhaps another hour passed before she abruptly made up her mind to set out to find herself something to eat.

She was fortunate that at the moment when she did this the little hall was empty. The door of the drawing-room still

stood open, but she was careful not to look through it and
so did not know if the dead still possessed the room, or if
they had been moved to the ambulance which she saw
outside the front door, which also stood open. Going to the
kitchen, she made herself a cheese sandwich and some
coffee. Looking at her watch then she saw that it was nearly
five o'clock.

Eating the sandwich and drinking the coffee, she began
to feel more normal than she had felt since coming back
into the house that morning. She would have liked to remove
the birthday cake from the table, to put it somewhere out
of sight so that she would not have to go on suffering the
horrible mockery of the hopeful message on it in its pretty
pink icing. But since the police had not moved it, she
presumed that they wanted it to stay where it was. They
could not want her to stay here much longer, she thought.
Soon she would be able to pack the small suitcase which
she had brought with her and make for home.

As she was thinking this, someone knocked at the back
door.

She went to open it. Conrad Greer stood there.

'In God's name, what's going on?' he asked in a hoarse
whisper, as if he was afraid of being overheard by someone
in the house.

'Of course, you don't know,' Constance said, the fact that
he was one of the people who certainly ought to know
occurring to her for the first time. 'Come in. What's that
you've got there?' She pointed at a cardboard box that he
was carrying carefully between both hands.

'Oh, it's just the chessmen for Colin,' he answered as he
stepped into the kitchen. 'I thought I'd bring them along
this evening so that they could be among his presents in the
morning. But what's wrong, Mrs Lawley? I went to
the door on the terrace, the way I usually come in, but the
french window was locked and there was no one in the
room, and then I saw a man come in and stand looking

round, someone I'd never seen before, and then I saw through the window across the room that there was an ambulance outside and some more men there. What's happened. Has Dorothea been taken ill again?'

'The chessmen for Colin!' Constance gasped. 'Oh God, it only needed that!'

He put the box down on the table beside the cake. 'Please tell me what's happened.' He was still half-whispering which somehow made it more difficult for Constance to speak calmly than it would have been if he had spoken normally.

Sitting down, leaning her head on her hands, she said, 'I haven't much experience of breaking bad news. I don't know how to set about it. But a fearful thing has happened. Colin somehow got hold of a gun this morning and he shot his grandparents and his mother and then, it seems, himself. Those men you saw out there are police. They've been here all day and if the drawing-room's empty now it's because they've put the bodies into the ambulance. I think they'll be leaving soon.'

'The bodies!' he exclaimed. 'Colin shot them? You mean he killed them?'

'Isn't that what I said?'

'Yes, but . . . You can't mean that. Why would Colin do a thing like that?'

'Why does a boy like Colin do anything?'

'You do mean it!' His voice was suddenly loud.

'Yes.'

'His grandparents and Margot?'

'Yes, yes, yes!' For the moment she felt wildly impatient with him because he was being so slow, taking it in. But then she recognized how hard it would have been for her to believe what had happened if she had not walked into the dreadful room and seen it for herself. When she spoke again her voice was gentle. 'He was your son, wasn't he?'

He nodded and seemed about to say something, but paused, then asked, 'Who's in charge here?'

'A man called Frayne.'

'I'd better go and talk to him.'

He turned towards the door, but as he did so it opened and Inspector Frayne came into the kitchen. Seeing Greer, he looked questioningly at Constance, waiting to have the presence of his man explained.

She said, 'This is Mr Greer, a neighbour.'

'Greer?' the Inspector said. 'Anything to do with the Greer who owns the antique shop in Bracklington?'

'Yes,' Greer said shortly.

'That's who you are? Come to think of it, someone told me you lived in Long Meldon, I can't remember who at the moment. What's this?' He put his hands on the cardboard box on the table.

'Leave that!' Greer said. 'It was just something for the boy's birthday. Please don't touch it.'

But Frayne had already lifted the lid and was looking into the box.

'Chessmen,' he said softly. 'That might be interesting.'

CHAPTER 5

For a moment after that neither of the men said anything. Frayne went on looking at the box. Greer looked at him with an expression of deep shock on his face. Then Frayne put the lid back on the box and picked it up.

Greer exclaimed, 'Leave that! It's nothing to do with you.'

'If that's true, it'll be returned to you undamaged,' Frayne said equably.

'You're meaning to take it away with you?' Greer asked.

'Probably.'

'I'm sure you've no right to do that. I'm sure you've no right. You don't believe it's got anything to do with this

ghastly thing that's happened here, do you? How could it?
I've only just heard about it.'

'All the same, it could be interesting.'

'Why?'

'The boy played chess, didn't he?'

'Yes.'

'And those were a present for him?'

'Yes, but I still don't understand why you want to take
them away. They're quite valuable, you know.'

'I rather thought they might be. Where did they come
from?'

'That's none of your business. I had them, I thought I'd
give them to him. But he's dead, so I'll take them home
again.'

The antagonism between the two men was quiet but
intense and to Constance it seemed to be growing. Shrinking
from it, feeling that Greer was incomprehensibly upset and
that an explosion resulting from this would be just more
than she could bear, she said, 'I wouldn't make a fuss about
it, Mr Greer. I don't know why Inspector Frayne wants
them, but I'm sure you'll get them back all right.'

'Thank you, Mrs Lawley,' Frayne said. 'I promise that.
But I'd like to know where you got them, Mr Greer.'

'They've been in my shop for some time,' Greer answered.
'I forget where I got them.'

'You bought them from someone, I suppose.'

'Naturally.'

'But you don't remember who?'

'No.'

'Don't you keep records of that sort of thing?'

'There's probably a record in my books in the shop, but
I don't carry it around in my head.'

'Well, I'll call in at the shop sometime. Perhaps you can
check your records meanwhile.'

'I suppose so,' Greer said grudgingly. 'But I still don't
understand why you're interested in them. Colonel Barrow

seemed to think they weren't the right sort of thing to give
a boy like Colin and I nearly changed my mind about giving
them to him, but I hadn't anything else and it was a bit
late to go shopping, so I took the risk of giving them to him
all the same.'

'Ah, so you thought there was some risk about doing it.'

It appeared to be another question to which Greer did
not immediately know the answer.

At length he said, in a more propitiatory tone than he
had yet used in this argument, 'I'm always scared about
giving presents. If you can see they aren't liked, if you've
made a blunder, choosing them, it can hurt quite a bit.
Colonel Barrow seemed to think Colin might not value them
and might even smash them.'

'But you didn't think he'd really do that, or you wouldn't
have brought them.'

'Just so.'

'All the same, you've known him to be violent, have you?
Has he smashed things before?'

'Colonel Barrow told me once about a teddy-bear he'd
cut up with a razor. But that was long ago. I've never seen
him violent myself.'

'Can you believe he killed his grandparents and his
mother?'

Greer seemed to take this question more calmly than he
had those about the chessmen. He moved towards a chair
and sat down, gazing before him with unfocused eyes
as if he hoped to find the answer in the empty air before
him.

'I've got to believe it, haven't I?' he said in a low voice.
'Mrs Lawley told me that's what happened. Is there any
other explanation possible?'

'It's still too soon to say,' Frayne answered. 'That's what
it looks like. But can you believe it of him?'

'I suppose so. If he was badly enough upset. He had very
unpredictable moods.'

'He seems to have been very upset by the arrival of his mother and the man I suppose one should call his stepfather.'

'Wouldn't any child be? He'd believed all his life his mother was dead.'

'But not every child would know where to lay his hands on a gun. Do you know if Colonel Barrow kept a gun in the house?'

'Yes, as it happens I do. He showed it to me once. I think it was a memento of his days in India.'

'So Colin probably knew about it.'

'He must have.'

'Yes, well, thank you, Mr Greer. It's useful to know about the gun. By the way, you've known the Barrows a long time, have you?'

'Oh yes.'

'Before they moved to Long Meldon?'

'Yes, as a matter of fact it was I who found them this house. They'd just taken on Colin and they talked to me about wanting to move into the country, as they thought it would be the best thing for him, and I happened to know this house was coming on to the market and I told them about it.'

'I see. Well, we'll be in touch again soon.' Suddenly moving rapidly, Frayne picked up the box of chessmen and almost as if he felt that Greer might follow and snatch it from him, shot out of the kitchen.

The moment he had gone Greer, startled by the swiftness of it, broke into an explosion of curses, which seemed to relate to the abduction of the chessmen rather than to anything else.

'But it doesn't really matter, does it?' Constance said. 'I suppose he's got to investigate everything that could conceivably have anything to do with Colin, but he'll soon see these couldn't possibly and he'll bring them back to you.'

Greer drew a deep breath and let it out slowly. He seemed to be making a deliberate effort to relax, yet when he looked at Constance she thought that there was still a strange gleam of fear in his eyes.

'I can't help wondering . . .' he began, then paused.

'Yes?' Constance said.

'No, it's absurd.' He drew a hand across his forehead, temporarily smoothing out the deep lines that had appeared there. 'I was just wondering if Godfrey could have told Colin about the chessmen and how he'd advised me not to give them to him, and could that have made Colin furious, because he wanted them. I think I showed them to him once when Dorothea brought him into the shop one day. She rather liked coming in and picking up knick-knacks. No, it's absurd.'

Constance thought that it was absurd too. Furthermore, she did not believe it was what Greer had started to say when he stated that there was something that he could not help wondering about. He could not even momentarily have imagined that the murderous impulse that had moved Colin had been prompted by the deprivation of some chessmen that he had fancied. She looked curiously at Greer, wondering what it was that he was trying so hard to hide. He had not told Frayne that he was Colin's father and that once, many years ago, he had had a close relationship with Margot Pauling. But that was something which in these days there was no great need to conceal.

He stood up, looking at the birthday cake, and said, 'I'd like to smash that bloody thing to pieces.'

'So would I, rather,' Constance said.

'Are you staying the night here?' he asked.

'No, I'm going home.'

'I dont blame you. Well, I'll be off home myself. If there's anything I can do, you'll let me know, won't you?'

'Thank you, yes. But I don't think they'll want me for anything more.'

'Goodbye, then.'

'Goodbye.'

He let himself out of the back door.

If Constance had not felt as tired as she did, she would have got up then and gone in search of Inspector Frayne to ask if there was any reason why she should remain in the house. The thought of her own home had never seemed so attractive. But lethargy, the aftermath of emotions to which she was wholly unaccustomed, kept her passively where she was.

She could not guess why the detective had been so interested in the chessmen and had so relentlessly taken possession of them. They seemed to her as irrelevant as the things that she had bought in the village that morning and which, she realized with slight surprise, she had not yet put away. Wearily she got up and started putting them into the refrigerator. But was there any point in bothering with this, she wondered. There was no one left in the house who would ever again be requiring food. In a little while everything in the refrigerator would have to be emptied into the dustbin. But wasting food was one of the things of which she was incapable.

She had just closed the door of the refrigerator on her purchases when Frayne came back into the kitchen.

She imagined that it would be to tell her that she could go home, but he said, 'You're wanted on the telephone.'

'*I* am?' she said, believing that there was no one who would think of telephoning her here. Then she wondered if it could be Pauling.

'Yes,' Frayne said. 'Will you take it in the dining-room?'

'While you listen in in the hall?'

'Do you mind?'

'You'd do it whether I mind or not, wouldn't you?' she said. 'And I imagine it's best for me if you do it. You'll know I haven't some secret ploy going on. But I wish I understood what you want with those chessmen.'

'Fingerprints, for one thing.'

'But what can they tell you? There'll be all sorts of people's prints on them, won't there?'

'That remains to be seen. But I shouldn't keep this lady on the telephone waiting.'

'It's a lady, is it?'

'That's right.'

She went to the dining-room, picked up the telephone and said, 'Constance Lawley speaking.'

'Oh, Mrs Lawley, this is Julie Hyland,' a voice said. 'I wanted to ask you about Jennifer. Is she with you?'

'No,' Constance replied.

'Has she been with you any time today?'

'No. But she came here in the morning. I know that because she delivered Colin's birthday cake. But I was out at the time.'

'But you're sure she did that?'

'Yes, it's here. It was she who delivered it, I suppose. It couldn't have been anyone else?'

'No, it must have been Jennifer. Anyway, she took it with her when she left here and I can't imagine she'd have handed it over to someone else to make the actual delivery. But you haven't seen her?'

'No. But, Miss Hyland, do you know about what's happened here today?'

There was a slight pause, then Julie's voice, with a slight shake in it, went on, 'Yes, the police came here this afternoon because they wanted to speak to Jennifer, and they told me the whole awful story. I believe it was you who walked in on it and found—everything. It must have been an unspeakable shock for you.'

'It was.'

'I'm—I'm so sorry—for you, I mean, and for all of them. But I always felt that boy Colin was sooner or later going to turn out to be dangerous. I didn't think anyone took his mental condition nearly seriously enough.'

'It looks as if you were right.'

'Nobody listened to me, though. They all knew he didn't like me and I suppose when I tried to warn them, as I did, they thought I was just getting my own back. I think it was really the other way round, I mean, that he didn't like me because he knew what I thought of him. Conrad adored the little horror. Of course, you know he was his son.'

'That's what Mr Pauling told me.'

'Oh, it's true. You'd only to look at them to see the resemblance. But about Jennifer, Mrs Lawley, actually I'm getting rather worried about her. It isn't at all like her to stay away for most of the day without telling me she was going to do it. Do you think I ought to tell the police about it?'

'I don't think there's any need to do that,' Constance said, 'because they're listening in on this line.'

'Oh!' There was a sound of shock in it, then there was a pause, as if Julie were trying to assess whether or not this mattered. Then she went on, 'That simplifies matters, of course. So they're still in the house with you.'

'Yes.'

'You're staying the night there, are you?'

'No, I'm going home.'

'I was hoping I could come up and have a talk with you. I've a feeling the police didn't tell me everything—and if they're listening in now and heard me say that, it doesn't matter, does it? How much longer will you be there?'

'I don't know. Anyway, I can wait for you if you want to come. There's something I'd rather like to ask you . . .' But the thought of the listener on the line checked her. 'Well, I can ask you about it when you get here.'

'I'll be along quite soon, then. Meanwhile, if you hear anything from Jennifer, you'll let me know, won't you?'

'Of course.'

Constance heard her ring off and put down the telephone that she was holding. The question that she had nearly asked Julie had concerned the chessmen. If they had come from the antique shop in Bracklington, Julie very probably knew where they had come from in the first place, and when Conrad Greer had removed them from the shop, and what connection, if any, they could have with the morning's crimes. She thought that Frayne was an intelligent man and that his interest in the chessmen could not be without significance, but what significance it had puzzled her very much and she did not like being puzzled.

The police left the house soon afterwards, Frayne telling Constance that she was free to go home when she liked, but that he would like her to be available there next day as he would still require a formal statement from her. She had been longing for all the men to leave, yet as soon as they had gone the emptiness and silence of the house became almost unbearable. She wished that she had not given Julie the promise to wait for her to come. If only she had thought faster she could have suggested that she would call in at Jenny's Café on her way home. Since Jennifer was more likely to return there than to come to Riverside it would really have been a far more sensible arrangement than to wait here. She might still do that, she thought. She could telephone the café and suggest to Julie that she should wait there for Constance to come.

When she telephoned, however, there was no reply. The café, she supposed, was already closed for the evening and Julie was on her way here, and only a moment after putting the telephone down Constance heard the front door bell ring. Going to answer it, she assumed that it would be Julie who was there, but with a slight start of surprise, she saw that it was Kenneth Pauling.

He noticed the start and said, 'I'm afraid you weren't expecting me. But may I come in? I know what happened to Margot and the others, but if you wouldn't mind . . . I know it sounds morbid, but I've an awful desire to see where it happened and to ask you a few things. But if you'd sooner I went away, I'll go.'

'It's only that I was expecting someone else,' Constance said, 'and that I'm meaning to go home as soon as I can. And I'm afraid you can't see the actual room where it happened, because they've put seals on the door. I suppose they mean to come back tomorrow, though I'm not sure what for. The whole tragic thing seems to be quite simple in its awful way. But come in and have a drink. I've no work to do this evening and I'm not in any hurry to go anywhere.'

He followed her inside, then stood still in the hall, looking at the closed door of the drawing-room.

'It was in there, was it?' he asked.

'Yes,' she answered. She hesitated for a moment, uncertain where to take him, then led him into the dining-room. The bottle of brandy from which she had helped herself in the morning, was still on the table. 'Brandy?' she said, 'or whisky, or sherry?'

'Whisky, please, with soda, if you've got it.' Going to the window, he stood there, gazing out. The daylight was beginning to lose its brilliance, though it was not yet dusk. Beyond the terrace a lawn sloped away between wide herbaceous borders towards a copse of beeches and the river Meldon. 'It looks so peaceful, doesn't it?' he said. 'It's hard to take in what's happened here. I told you I knew about it. The police came to see me this afternoon, asked me questions about my relationship with Margot, then wanted me to go to the morgue to identify her. I've been walking round in a sort of daze ever since. Do you think it would have happened if I hadn't come here? Was it my coming that pushed the boy over the edge?'

Constance poured out whisky for him and after some hesitation a small brandy for herself. Even that, she thought, might be unwise, since she was intending to drive into Bracklington shortly, and as she had had hardly anything to eat all day, the drink, she knew, would go to her head. But she wanted it badly and thought that after all, if she felt unsure of herself, she could stay overnight in this house. Now that the police had gone and she was becoming more used to the silence of the place, the idea of staying there no longer seemed so frightening.

'It's useless to ask oneself that sort of question,' she said. 'A little while ago I was asking myself if it was my fault because I didn't take Colin seriously when he told me he meant to kill everybody. Perhaps it was my fault, but blaming myself now isn't going to help anybody.'

He turned towards the table and picked up the whisky and soda that she had poured out for him.

'I suppose there's no doubt it was the boy who killed them all,' he said.

'I don't think there's any question of it,' she answered.

'Somehow I can't believe it.'

'Oh, I've that feeling too. Really terrible things only happen to other people, don't they? One doesn't get involved in them oneself.'

'I suppose there's no one else who had any motive to kill them all,' he said.

She wrinkled her forehead, looking at him, wondering how serious he was. He did not meet her eyes, but looked down at his drink. His square face had a closed, aloof expression on it.

'I can't imagine anyone wanting to kill Colonel and Mrs Barrow except for some utterly irrational reason,' she said. 'They were quiet, kind people. I'm sure they never did anyone any harm in their lives. And they weren't rich. Comfortably off, but not affluent. I don't know of anyone who stood to inherit much by their deaths. I suppose at present-day prices this house alone is worth a good deal, but Colonel Barrow's pension will stop. Perhaps they had a certain amount in investments, but actually, since Margot and Colin are both dead too, I don't know who will inherit.'

'You know, it might be me,' Pauling said, still looking at his drink with that air of abstraction, then suddenly gulping half of it.

'You? Oh, because they may have left their money to Margot, and she may have made a will, leaving what she had to you?'

He nodded. 'She did that. We both made wills, leaving everything we had to each other.'

'But suppose the Barrows left everything they had to Colin.'

'Oh yes, I'm not thinking of making a claim to their property. All the same, it may come to me, and if I'd heard that it would, it would have given me a possible motive for killing the two old people, along with Margot and Colin. And as it happens, I'm in need of money.'

'I thought you had a good job in Sydney,' Constance said.

'So I had until a month ago, when the firm I've been working for went bust. And so far I haven't been able to find anything else. And Margot's business never made much money. It was more something to give her an interest than really a paying proposition.'

'What was it exactly?'

'Interior decorating. She was pretty gifted at it and from time to time she'd pull off a big deal and suddenly be flush. But it was nothing to count on.'

'Who's looking after it now?'

'An assistant she had, I presume, unless she simply walked out on it. A young woman who came into the business a couple of years ago. But I don't think she's experienced enough to take it over and I certainly couldn't, and if we simply sell up our stock it won't bring in much. Oh, I could do with a couple of hundred thousand, which I imagine is the sort of sum this house will fetch. Don't you think it's fortunate for me that I've got an alibi for the time of the killings?'

He looked up to meet her eyes now with a humourless smile.

'Are you thinking of our having coffee together around the time they happened?' Constance asked.

'You're a little quick for me, but yes, that had occurred to me,' he said.

'And that's why you really came up here this evening. It was to make sure I'd corroborate that.'

'Actually, no. It was only when you began to talk about the person who was going to inherit the Barrows' money that I realized it might be me and that that gave me a motive for wiping out the family. And so I thought of that coffee we had together and felt rather glad we'd had it.'

'What did you do after we separated?'

'I went for a stroll through the village, then went back to the Green Dragon and had a drink, then some lunch—' He stopped abruptly and the thick eyebrows over his light brown eyes twitched frowningly together. 'Look, you aren't seriously asking me for my alibi, are you?'

'It was you who introduced the subject,' she said.

'True, but I was merely exploring it theoretically, seeing if a case could be made out against me if the police should start to wonder if Colin really committed all those murders.'

'But I can't really support your alibi, you know.' The brandy was giving Constance a feeling that she was thinking remarkably clearly. 'When I left you I went into the grocer's and I was there quite a long time. And the murders are supposed to have happened only a very short time before I got in, so if you'd set off for this house immediately after we parted, you just might have been able to get here and carry out the shootings before I arrived.'

'Seems to me I'd have had to walk at a hell of a pace, which would probably have attracted attention to me as I went. There'd be witnesses to tell the police about it, but I'm not really afraid of them. I've no car, you know. I'd have had to come on foot.'

'But you didn't talk to anyone after you left me? There's no one who'd be able to say for sure where you were?'

He gave a harsh little laugh. 'I wonder if this is a rehearsal for the questions the police may be asking me tomorrow. If so, it may be useful. I realize I'd better do some thinking.'

'You know, you still haven't told me your real reason for coming here this evening,' Constance said. 'Was it really to have a look at the room where it all happened?'

He did not answer at once, but leaning his head on a hand, let his frown disappear and a look of faint amusement take its place.

'You're in the wrong job, aren't you?' he said. 'Someone like you could be very useful to the police. No, it wasn't really to have a look at the room. It was mainly to talk to you. I'd got to talk to someone. I tried sitting in my room with a book, but I couldn't bear it, so I thought I'd come here and perhaps you'd offer me a drink, as you did, and we could chat for a time and things wouldn't seem so awful and impossible as they were doing. But on the whole it seems to have been a mistake. This chat hasn't been exactly reassuring.'

'But it's you who made out the case against yourself—' she broke off as the door bell rang.

He quickly emptied his glass and stood up.

'If that's the police again . . .'

'I don't think it is,' Constance said. 'I think it's Miss Hyland. If you remember, we met her in the café this morning. She's worried about her sister.'

She left the dining-room and went to open the front door.

Julie Hyland stood there. She did not look as stern and self-assured as she had in the morning and the fair hair that then had been sleekly drawn back from her face had a wind-blown look, although there was no wind blowing that evening. It might be that she had been thrusting her fingers through it. She had on a light jacket over her cotton dress and had her hands thrust down into its pockets.

'Have you any news?' she asked.

'About Jennifer? No,' Constance answered. 'But why should you think I might have? Why should she come here?'

'I don't know. I don't know anything. I don't suppose she would. It's just that I'm feeling scared and more than a bit desperate. I feel I ought to be doing something. Don't you think I ought to tell the police that she still hasn't come home?'

'Well, come in,' Constance said. 'Join Mr Pauling and me in a drink. None of us knows what we ought to be doing. I think the answer is, nothing. But come in.'

Julie Hyland stepped into the hall and followed Constance to the dining-room. Pauling was standing where Constance had left him. He gave Julie a slightly puzzled scrutiny, as if he knew that they had met before, but could not for the moment remember where.

Then his face cleared and he said, 'Ah yes, this morning in the café.'

Constance introduced them. 'Miss Hyland—Mr Pauling. What will you have to drink, Miss Hyland?'

'For God's sake, call me Julie. Whisky, please.' Julie sank into a chair, sitting limply there as if she were very tired, yet looking at Pauling as if something about him were deeply interesting to her.

'You're Margot's husband,' she said as Constance put a glass of whisky in front of her.

'Yes,' he said.

'Then what's happened is very terrible for you. Specially terrible.'

'I think you may say that.'

Constance gave Pauling some more whisky and poured out some more brandy for herself. As she did it she made up her mind that she would not drive home that evening. The brandy was very comforting. It made her feel that there was nothing seriously wrong with her world. And that meant, she thought, that she could not be really fit to be on the road.

Julie turned to her.

'I can't understand it,' she said. 'Jennifer went off this morning to deliver Colin's cake. I thought she was going to come straight back. Then at first, when she didn't come, I thought she must have stayed here to have coffee and a chat with Mrs Barrow. And even when she didn't come home in time for lunch, I thought she might have stayed on, or met some other friend perhaps. But when the police came and told me what had happened here, I really began to worry. You see, it isn't like Jennifer to go off without any idea when she'd be back, and if for some reason she'd suddenly decided to go into Bracklington, shopping, or something of that sort, she'd probably have telephoned. But it's getting late now and she still hasn't come home. So what can I do about it?'

'Just why did the police come to see you this afternoon?' Pauling asked. 'Why did they connect you with things here?'

'Because of the cake, of course,' Julie answered. 'It was Jennifer they wanted to see, not me. They knew she'd been here because the cake had been delivered, and I suppose they wanted to know if she'd seen anything unusual.'

'And do you think she had?' he asked.

'How on earth can I tell?' Her voice rose momentarily with the shrillness of hysteria in it, but then she carefully controlled it and in a level tone went on, 'I can't help thinking it looks like it. But even if she did, why did she have to vanish? Suppose she actually saw that boy Colin shoot everyone and then himself and she couldn't stop him, why didn't she simply ring the police immediately? She'd have no reason to run away.'

'Shock, perhaps,' he suggested.

She gave a bewildered frown. 'Is that really possible?'

'I believe it might be,' he said. 'If she saw something as terrible as what happened, she might have had a complete black-out and be wandering around, not knowing where she is or even who she is.'

'She was in her car,' Julie said. 'The police didn't find it here, so she must have driven away in it. And she'd have had her handbag with her and there'd have been her banker's card in it and her cheque-book and so on, so when she came to she could have checked up . . . Oh, you think perhaps she hasn't come to yet! If there's any possibility of that I've got to get in touch with the police and tell them she still hasn't come home, haven't I?'

'I think I would,' Constance said.

'Can I use that telephone there?'

'Yes, go ahead.'

But Julie did not rise immediately to go to the telephone. Sipping her whisky, she looked thoughtfully at Pauling.

'You and your wife were the Paulings in Sydney who sometimes bought antiques from Conrad Greer, were you?'

'Did Margot do that?' he asked. 'I didn't know anything about that side of her business. She certainly got some very nice pieces from Europe from time to time.'

'Oh yes, it was one of my jobs to see to the despatching of them, but the name Pauling didn't mean anything to me. I didn't connect it with a daughter of the Barrows. But your wife was an old friend of Conrad's, wasn't she?'

'So I believe.' His tone was expressionless.

'But you didn't know she was still in contact with him. Oh yes, she was a good customer of ours. I work for him, you know. Now if you don't mind, Mrs Lawley, I'll telephone.'

Julie got up and went to the telephone, picked up the directory and looked for the number of the Bracklington police. When she had dialled and was answered, she said that she wanted to report a missing person. She spoke calmly, identifying herself, explaining her connection with the murders in Long Meldon and her fear that her sister might have seen them and in a state of shock be wandering about, suffering from loss of memory. Constance, listening, realized that at a certain point Julie had been connected with Detective-Inspector Frayne, for after a slight break she started repeating all that she had already said.

When she put the telephone down she said, 'They're putting out an alert, or whatever they call it, about her. I suppose they'll find her. Meanwhile there doesn't seem to be anything more I can do. I may as well go home. Thank you for listening to me, Mrs Lawley. Do you want a lift back to the village, Mr Pauling? I've got my car here.'

'Thank you,' he said, 'if it isn't any trouble to you.'

'Shall we go, then?'

He and Julie left together. Constance, who by then had decided to stay the night in the house, went to the front door with them and closed it after them. It disturbed her in a way that she did not understand to see them walking together towards Julie's car. From the moment when Julie had spoken of Margot buying antiques from Conrad Greer and Pauling had answered her so flatly, she had felt that there was something between them, some kind of secret knowledge perhaps and certainly hostility, which brought a complexity into their relationship about which she did not want to have to think just then.

She did not want to think about anything at all. She wanted to finish her brandy, find something to eat for her supper and go to bed. Finding some cold lamb in the refrigerator, she cut up a tomato and made a slice of bread and butter, and listlessly and only half aware of what she was doing, sat down at the kitchen table, ate her snack and then went wearily upstairs. Within a few minutes of getting into bed she was in a deep and dreamless sleep.

The sound of the telephone ringing woke her.

At first she was only drowsily aware of it and because she was a guest in a house that belonged to other people, did not feel that there was any need for her to answer it. Then remembrance of the day before came flooding back, and grabbing her dressing-gown and struggling into it as she went, she hurried down the stairs to the telephone in the hall. But the ringing had stopped by the time that she reached it.

Sleepily she went into the kitchen and made coffee. Why on earth, she wondered, had she stayed on the evening before instead of going home. The real reason for it, she supposed, was that she had simply not felt up to it. The brandy had been part of it, but most of it had been nervous exhaustion. But there was no real reason why she should not go home this morning. She had just started on her second cup of coffee when the telephone rang again.

'Is that you, Mum?' a voice said when she answered. 'This is Irene.'

'Irene? Goodness me, how did you know where I was?' Constance asked.

'You wrote to me, remember?' Irene said. 'I got the letter yesterday morning.'

'I didn't know the Royal Mail did anything as fast as that nowadays,' Constance said. 'One wouldn't expect you to have got my letter till tomorrow at the earliest.'

'It is a bit surprising,' Irene agreed. 'But look, is it true you're in the house where that fearful massacre happened? Riverside—you mean you're really in a house called River- side, do you?'

There was a degree of concern in Irene's voice to which Constance was not accustomed.

'Yes, but how did you know about that?' she asked.

'It was on the seven o'clock news. I didn't believe it. Then I thought I'd better ring up and find out. Mum, it sounds terrible. Aren't you terrified?'

'Fairly terrified, yes,' Constance answered, 'though it's stupid because I wasn't even in the house when it happened and it's all over now except for the police coming and going. Was that you trying to phone me a little while ago?'

'Yes, and when I didn't get an answer I rang the house

in Bracklington, in case you'd gone home since you wrote, and then when I got no answer I thought I'd try this number again in case there'd been something wrong with the line, or you were having a bath or something. You're all right, are you, Mum? I mean, the shock must have been fearful and after all you aren't used to that kind of thing.'

'I can't say I've ever experienced anything quite like it before,' Constance said, 'but I think I've managed to keep my head.'

'That's fine. I mean, I knew you would, because you always keep your head in almost any circumstances, but I'm glad you've been able to face things. Living the sort of life you do, knowing from one day to the next just what's going to happen, it must have been specially shattering.'

'One never knows what's going to happen tomorrow, however humdrum one's existence seems to be. But you think your rather different experience of life would have fitted you to cope with the situation better than me.'

'Now don't go all sarcastic on me, Mum,' Irene said. 'Of course not. I'd have run from the house screaming, whereas I'm sure you did the proper thing and dialled 999. But I'm so afraid you'll pay for it later. I mean, keeping your head in a crisis often means that you'll feel ten times worse later on than if you let your feelings rip at the time. Not that I don't admire you for being able to do it. But I think I'd better come down in case you need some help presently. You'll be staying on at that house in Long Meldon, will you?'

'Now, please, Irene,' Constance said quickly, 'don't think of coming down. It's very sweet of you to think of it, but I really don't need any help.'

She certainly did not need any help, she thought, of the kind that Irene could give her.

'Oh, that's all right,' Irene said. 'I'll come. I'm not sure what the trains are, but I'll go to Paddington and take the

next one. Sunday trains are pretty bad, but I expect I'll
arrive some time this morning.'

'Please, Irene, don't . . . I'm not even sure if I'll be
staying here.'

'Don't worry about that. If you aren't at Long Meldon
I'll go on into Bracklington. I can afford a taxi. I've got
quite a lot of money, because I've got a job. And I really
don't like the thought of you having to cope with the police
all by yourself. Have they been awful?'

'The police?'

'Yes.'

'The man in charge here has been very courteous and
considerate.'

'That's what they're sometimes like to begin with. You
don't know what may happen next. Well, I'll be down later
this morning and meanwhile try not to get too depressed
and all that sort of thing.'

Constance heard the click of the telephone being put
down.

'Oh dear . . .' she murmured. She was not sure if she
felt more touched at Irene's unexpected concern for her,
astonished at the statement that she had a job, or appalled
at the thought of her interfering in Constance's quite good
relationship with Inspector Frayne.

Her next ordeal was the Press. She had just got dressed
when they started arriving. They came with notebooks, with
cameras, with questions, some of them putting to her the
one that she had always thought most supremely impertinent when she had heard it on radio or television. How had
she *felt*, they wanted to know, when she had walked into a
room and found four dead bodies in it. She tried replying
that she considered her feelings strictly private and thought
that ought to put an end to the matter, but the questions
came again and again, what had been her *feelings* when she
discovered the tragedy. Shock, she admitted now, wanting
at any price to be left to herself, terrible shock, and added

that she really had no words in which to express what she had felt. They nodded and scribbled in their notebooks and exuded a little synthetic sympathy, but seemed satisfied and strolled off. Thinking that they had really had no need to interview her at all, because they could safely have made up for themselves anything that she had told them, she closed the door on them, went up to her bedroom and began to pack her suitcase.

The front doorbell rang.

She was not much surprised to find Inspector Frayne on the doorstep. She had felt that she had not seen the last of him.

'So you stayed after all,' he said as he stepped into the hall.

'Yes, but I'm going home now, if you don't mind,' she said.

'Well, I'm not sure,' he said as she took him into the dining-room. 'It might be a good thing if you stayed on. But it's up to you to decide. It's just that it looks at the moment as if you may be about the last person to have seen Jennifer Hyland alive.'

'Alive?' she exclaimed. 'You don't mean . . .'

'I'm afraid I do,' he said. 'We found her this morning. If you go straight on up this lane past Mr Greer's house, you come a mile or so further on to a place where the river widens into a small pool. And a man coming down the lane about eight o'clock this morning noticed a car among the trees there, and because there's no track or any obvious reason why a car should be parked where it was, he went to take a look at it. It was empty, but there was a body in the pool. Drowned, he thought. Suicide. But it's turned out that she'd been violently struck on the head before she drowned, so after all the probability is that it's murder.'

CHAPTER 6

Constance was shocked at the first thought that came into her mind as she listened. It was that in her last job, where her employers had objected to all food that was not grown organically and to eggs that had not been laid by freerange fowls, there had been no hint of violence in their home, no mystery, no murder. Trying to do the housekeeping of a kind that they would accept had at times been difficult, but how peaceful it had been, how secure it had felt.

'But why?' she said.

'Why was she murdered?'

'Yes.'

'There are several possible reasons,' Frayne answered. He dropped into a chair at the table and sat there in the drooping attitude of extreme weariness. Constance wondered if he had had any sleep that night. 'One, did she pick up a hitch-hiker who killed her, stole her handbag and made off? However, she hadn't been raped, that's one thing we know.'

'But her handbag's missing, is it?' Constance said.

'Yes, but we found it in a ditch at the edge of the lane, with only the money she'd had in it missing.'

'Was she carrying much money?'

'We've been talking to her sister and she thinks probably not. But that doesn't necessarily mean anything. Murders have been done for as little as thirty pence.'

'What other reasons are there?'

'There's the one that stares one in the face. She came here with the birthday cake, saw something and had to be put out of the way.'

Constance, who had sat down facing him, felt a chill go through her.

'That doesn't make sense, does it?' she said. 'If Jennifer saw Colin shooting his grandparents and his mother and then himself, he couldn't have done her any harm, could he?'

'No,' he agreed. 'If you put it like that, probably not.'

'Why only probably not? Why not certainly not?' She looked searchingly into his bright blue eyes which this morning looked duller than she had yet seen them. 'What do you really believe?'

'If you want to hide a leaf,' he said, 'where would you put it?'

'Oh, I know the answer to that one—in a forest,' she replied.

'And if you want to hide a corpse?'

'On a battlefield, I presume.'

'But suppose there's no convenient little war going on in your neighbourhood, what then?'

Her gaze on his tired face changed from being merely curious to suddenly intent and more than a little scared.

'I think I understand what you mean,' she said. 'You suspect that at least one of the people in that room yesterday wasn't killed by Colin. That someone who saw what Colin was doing took the opportunity of adding another corpse to the slaughter. And Jennifer saw it happen.'

'Well, what do you think of it?' he asked.

She shut her eyes, trying to visualize what might have happened in the pleasant drawing-room while she had been out shopping. It might have been something even more horrific and much more bewildering than she had yet imagined.

'I can think of one argument against it,' she said after a long pause.

'I'd be glad to hear it.'

'It's a question of time. I think it was about half past ten when I went to Jenny's Café to have a cup of coffee with Mr Pauling. And as we went in we saw Jennifer setting out in her car. Her sister Julie says she believed Jennifer was just going to deliver the cake here . . . Oh God!' She stopped.

'What is it?' Frayne asked.

'Just that I've remembered today was Colin's birthday. The cake and the chessmen and I believe a camera were all for him. I hadn't thought of that till this moment.'

'It isn't the pleasantest of thoughts. But what were you going to say about Jennifer Hyland delivering the cake?'

'Only that if she'd come straight here she'd have arrived at, say, a quarter to eleven at the latest. But I believe your people think the murders happened only very shortly before I got in and that can't have been much before half past eleven at the very earliest. I told you, after Mr Pauling and I had had our coffee I did some shopping and I took quite a time about it. So if Jennifer saw something like a murder done by someone who wasn't Colin and was killed because of what she'd seen, what was she doing between the time she got here and the time the murders were done? If she'd simply been sitting here, chatting to Mrs Barrow when the shootings began, she'd have been killed here too, wouldn't she? She wouldn't have been driven up the lane and hit over the head and drowned in a pool there, at great risk, I'd say, to whoever did it. She'd simply have been left in the carnage here.'

He nodded. 'I thought you'd say that.'

'Doesn't it make sense?'

'Oh yes. Yes, very much so. And it means it's important to account for what she was doing for about the half hour or so after you saw her drive away from the café. We've got men out, making inquiries about that now. The answer may be something quite simple, for instance, that she dropped in on a friend for a chat before she came up here and so just happened to be on the spot when the extra murder happened.'

'You're really sure there was an extra murder, are you?'

'Oh no, not sure.'

'But it's what you believe, isn't it?'

'I'm inclined to believe it. But it could have been something else she saw, not a murder. For instance, someone
might have been looking on and saw the murders were going
to happen and didn't interfere. That could be a very serious
criminal offence. Someone might even have encouraged
the boy to do what we think he did. If she was a witness
to that it might be worth that person's while to get rid of
her.'

'They'd have had to see it through the french window on
to the terrace, wouldn't they?'

'That's probable.'

'And the person who had a way of coming in and out of
the house that way was Conrad Greer. And you've im-
pounded his chessmen. That still puzzles me. Have they
told you anything?'

'Only that they were stolen.'

'Stolen!' She drew a deep breath, let it out in a slow sigh
and shook her head. 'I don't understand. Do you mean by
Conrad Greer?'

'Oh, not necessarily,' he said. 'He may have bought them
in good faith. Buying stolen goods is one of the risks all
antique dealers run. His deciding to give them as a present
to the boy suggests that he didn't know they were stolen. If
he had known it, he'd have realized what a risk he was
running, doing it.'

'How do you know they were stolen?'

'There are some fingerprints on several of the pieces which
indicate that they were formerly the property of a certain
Lady Bancroft who lives in Granwich, that village about
ten miles the other side of Bracklington. You probably know
it. Last May she had a burglary in her house there in which,
among other things, all of them reasonably valuable, a set
of Chinese chessmen were stolen. We're fairly sure who took
them and even what he did with them, and that was why I
took possession of them when I saw them here.'

'You say you're fairly sure what this person did with
them.'

'Of course, one can be wrong.'

'But all the same, you're suspicious he sold them to
Conrad Greer and that he knew what he was doing, buying
them. In other words, he's a fence.'

'Is that what you think yourself?'

'It's what you think, isn't it?'

'I wouldn't go so far as to say that.'

'Because it would be very indiscreet if you haven't enough
evidence. But I think you believe he's a fence and perhaps
that his shop is only a front for other activities, and you're
about ready to pounce on him for it any time now. I'd like
to know if you think the Paulings are involved.'

'The Paulings?' he said with raised eyebrows. He looked
unable to follow her.

'Yes, both of whom are here now,' she said. 'One dead,
one alive. And who, according to Julie Hyland, were good
customers of Conrad Greer's. Margot Pauling ran an interior decorating business in Sydney, and a supply of good
antiques from Europe may have been very useful to her.
But did she know that what she was getting had been stolen?
Apart from that, suppose you tell me something else. Why
did you come to see me this morning?'

He gave a slight shrug of his shoulders.

'Partly to have the sort of talk we've been having. That's
to say, to find out if you knew anything that might be useful,
even if you hadn't realized it yourself. Like this Pauling
connection, for instance. No doubt we'd have got around to
that ourselves fairly soon, but I think you've saved us some
trouble. I've been thinking of the Paulings only in terms of
the break-up of their marriage. Since we began to think that
at least one of the deaths in that room might not have been
the work of Colin, who was the likeliest victim? And I was
inclined to think it was Margot Pauling and that possibly
her husband was the murderer, with the simple motive of

revenge for her having left him. But if she and her husband
were in contact with Greer and know how his deliveries to
them had been come by, perhaps Greer himself had a motive
for wanting her dead. If she threatened him, perhaps, after
getting here. Even tried to blackmail him.'

She shook her head. 'I still can't make sense of it. I suppose
Mr Pauling could have come here after we separated in
the village and got here in time to murder his wife before I
got back. And I suppose Mr Greer could have come here
any time while I was out shopping and shot Mrs Pauling.
But how could either of them have known that there'd be a
gun available? How could they have known about that leaf
in the forest, or that corpse on the battlefield? How could
they have known that there'd be a possibility of leaving a
body among a few other bodies, so that Colin would be
blamed? They couldn't have known it, could they?'

'No,' he agreed, 'they couldn't. So whoever came here
came without any intention of committing a murder. They
came for some other reason. Then seeing Colin with a gun,
shooting his grandparents, then himself, they couldn't resist
the opportunity it gave of shooting Margot Pauling and
adding her body to the slaughter.'

'But he was seen by Jennifer Hyland, and so had to
dispose of her too.'

'That's how it looks.'

'You said she was struck on the head before she was
drowned. Do you know what she was struck with?'

'Not for sure. There are men out hunting around the
place where she was found to see if they can find a weapon.
But there's one thing I can tell you about that. We noticed
something unusual in the drawing-room here yesterday.
The set of fire irons in the fireplace isn't complete. There
are a shovel and a pair of tongs, but no poker. The blows
on her head could have been inflicted by a poker.'

Constance found herself doing something that she had
been trying to avoid for the last twenty-four hours. It was

visualizing the scene in the drawing-room as it had been when she had walked in the morning before. She realized now that she had had hardly more than a glimpse of it. She had run from the room so quickly that she found it difficult to be sure that her memory of it was accurate. It seemed to her that what she had seen had been so deeply impressed on her brain that she would never forget it, yet how could she be certain of that?

'If you're right,' she said slowly, picking her words, 'then Margot Pauling wasn't in the room when Colin shot his grandparents. If she had been, she'd have been his first target, wouldn't she?'

'That seems likely for more than one reason,' Frayne agreed.

'For more than one?'

'Yes, there's the obvious one that she'd have been what you called his first target because he probably hated her more than anybody, except perhaps his stepfather. His hatred for his grandparents appears to have been because of all the lies they'd told him about his mother, but she was the one who'd abandoned him and had no love for him. But there's some other evidence that she was on the terrace when Colin began his shooting. There's an ashtray on the table there with two or three cigarette stubs in it and the remains of a cigarette that had burnt itself out, only half-smoked. What it looks like is that she was sitting out there smoking when Colin began his murders, then when she heard the shots she dropped her cigarette in the ashtray and came running into the room to see what was happening and got shot herself.'

'But not by Colin?'

'Really we aren't sure. There are only his fingerprints on the gun and it was in just the place where it would have fallen from his hand beside him when he'd shot himself. If I could think of any reason why Jennifer Hyland should be murdered except that she'd seen something that was very

dangerous to someone, I'd feel inclined to think that Colin
was responsible for all the other murders.'

A sense of acute tension made Constance suddenly restless
and getting up she went to the window and stood looking
out at the terrace. That was where Colin had loved to play
chess and where today he ought to have been proudly setting
up his chessmen and inducing Conrad Greer to play with
him. Conrad Greer who had almost certainly acquired
the chessmen knowing them to have been stolen and who
perhaps had shot the woman who had borne his son. If
Colin had known only half of it, it would not have been
astonishing that he should have gone berserk.

The terrace was where Margot Pauling had been sitting
when she had heard the shooting begin. And she had dashed
in to see what was happening instead of removing herself
immediately to safety. A brave woman, even if there was
not much else to be said in her favour.

'You know, you still haven't really told me why you
wanted to see me this morning,' Constance said. 'You said
it was partly to talk about the matter in general, but wasn't
there some other reason too?'

'Well, I wanted to ask you about that poker,' he said.
'You've been in and out of that room a number of times
since you first came here, I suppose. Did you ever notice if
there was a poker as well as a shovel and tongs?'

She turned and went back to her chair at the table.

'No, I didn't,' she said. 'At this time of year you don't
think about fires. I saw that there was a fire laid on the
hearth so that they could light it if it got chilly in the
evening, but I didn't notice the fire irons.'

'So if they didn't have a poker there before all this
happened, we've got to look for some other weapon,' Frayne
said.

'But if the poker was the weapon, it means Jennifer was
attacked in this house.'

'I think so, yes.'

'And then carried to her car and driven away. Wouldn't that have needed a good deal of strength?'

'Yes, I should say a fair amount.'

'I wish I knew what you really think about it all.'

'So do I.' He stood up. 'It might help. Are you going home now?'

'I don't think so,' she answered. 'My daughter's coming down, as I understand it to give me some moral support. She'll be coming here, so I'll wait at least until she gets here.'

'You've a family, have you?'

'A son and a daughter. My son's farming in New Zealand, my daughter—well, she lives in London.'

'And you take on this kind of job quite frequently?'

'Not exactly this kind, as it's turned out.'

'No, of course not. But you must run into some pretty strange situations sometimes, all the same.'

'Fewer than you'd think. Most people are abysmally normal, or at least put up a show of being so as long as I'm around. *Pas devant les domestiques*, you know.'

'Ah,' he said. 'I suppose I know what that means. Tell me, would you say that Jennifer Hyland was one of the normal, abysmal or otherwise?'

She stood up too and together they moved towards the door.

'Now why should you ask me that?' she said.

'Only that we just could have been thinking about the whole thing the wrong way up. Suppose it was she who committed all the murders after delivering the birthday cake and was killed by someone who saw her do it. I can see certain arguments against that. How did she know there was a gun in the house? How did she know where it was kept? How did she lay her hands on it? And why might she have done it? Why? You've been living here in the house for a few days. Can you think of any reason why Jennifer Hyland might have wanted to exterminate the family?'

'So that's what you really came to ask me?' Constance said.

They had reached the closed front door and now stood still before it. Constance's hand was on the latch, but she did not turn it.

'Well, can you?' he asked.

'I can't think of anyone who'd have wanted to do that,' she said.

'Can you think of any single one of them she might have wanted to kill? Margot Pauling, for instance?'

'Because . . .' She paused, trying to think of the implications of this new approach. 'Because, say, she was in love with Conrad Greer and was afraid that Margot might take him away from her? And he saw her do it and killed her in fury at what she'd done?'

'Have you seen any sign that she and Greer had any interest in one another?'

'I've never even seen them together.'

'Ah well,' he said, sounding reluctant to give up a theory that had attracted him. 'I'll have to stick to it that Colin killed his grandparents, but Jennifer must have seen something, you know, so it seems to me most probable that that was the shooting of Margot. Thank you for listening to me. I still need that formal statement from you. If you'll come into the police station later in the day, we'll settle that.'

Constance opened the door for him and he went out.

As she closed the door behind him, she said aloud, her voice sounding strange and echoing in the empty house, 'He can't have meant that. He can't have thought Jennifer killed off the family. He didn't. So what did he mean? The man isn't a fool.'

It was at nearly half past twelve that Irene arrived at the house. A taxi brought her. She got out of it with a suitcase and a large, curiously shaped object, the nature of which Constance could not guess at. She saw Irene and the taxi

from the window of her bedroom, to which she had returned
to finish her small amount of packing. Irene put her finger
on the door bell and left it there until, Constance presumed,
she heard footsteps on the staircase and knew that someone was coming to let her in. Giving up the ringing then,
Irene was standing with the suitcase in one hand and the
unidentified object in the other, ready to enter.

She came in, put both things down in the hall and kissed
Constance.

'You look all right,' Irene said in a faintly reproving tone,
as if there were something improper about her mother
looking all right after what she had been through. 'I always
forget how tough people like you can be. It's astonishing
when you come to think of it. I mean, when you've led such
a sheltered life and had so little experience. But I'm so glad
you've survived so well.'

Irene was a tall girl, slender and well-proportioned, with
chestnut hair to her shoulders and big, greenish eyes. Her
features were delicate, her skin pale and clear. Whenever
Constance met her after a fairly long interval she was always
taken by surprise at how very good-looking Irene was.

Normally she did nothing to encourage such a view of
her. Her usual dress was jeans and a T-shirt, she never wore
make-up and never dreamed of having her really beautiful
hair attended to by a hairdresser. Today, however, she was
in a pretty pale grey dress, subdued, but for her amazingly
elegant, was wearing long gold earrings and had a slightly
excessive amount of make-up around her eyes, which made
them look very large and brilliant. Constance wondered if
this might all be in honour of murder. Was it Irene's idea
of the formality due to such an unusual and important
occasion?

'Whatever is that?' Constance asked, pointing to the
object that Irene had put down beside her suitcase. It was
the case of a musical instrument, Constance had recognized,
but of what kind she could not guess.

'It's a French horn,' Irene answered. 'I've just taken it up.'

'What made you do that?'

'Well, someone told me it's the most difficult instrument to play that there is,' Irene answered, 'and I thought that was a challenge.'

'Doesn't it interfere with your chanting?'

'I've given that up. I wasn't getting anywhere with it.'

'So you won't be wanting to do any while you're here. That's a relief. But are you still living in that community?'

'No, I've moved out. I've got a flat of my own now. I told you I'd got a job, didn't I? It's in a bookshop. I'm rather enjoying it.' Irene said this with a kind of surprise, as if the idea of enjoying a job were something astonishing.

'But then how did you get my letter?' Constance asked. 'I addressed it to you at your old address.'

'A friend of mine who sometimes calls in there brought it to me,' Irene said. 'Actually he's going to move into my flat later today. I left the keys with him. We're thinking of getting married.'

'Now this is a bit too much of a good thing,' Constance said. 'You're looking all clean and tidy and as pretty as can be, you've got a job you like and you're thinking of getting married. I can't believe it.'

Irene put an arm round her and kissed her again.

'Take it easy, Mum,' she said. 'You know you're awfully pleased about it all.'

'I admit the French horn somewhat reassures me,' Constance said. 'As long as you're doing something really absurd I feel you're still the girl I know.'

'There's nothing absurd about a French horn,' Irene said austerely.

'But there is about your taking it up. You've never been in the least musical.'

'One can always develop, can't one? Perhaps I never had the right sort of encouragement. Look, have we got to stay out here in the hall? Can't we go and sit down somewhere and perhaps have a drink?'

'Come in here,' Constance said and led the way to the dining-room. 'I've been drinking more than really agrees with me. I only stayed here last night because I was feeling a bit drunk and was afraid of driving. What would you like?'

'What I really like is damson gin,' Irene said. 'There's a chap in the community who makes it. It's fabulous. But I don't suppose you've got any.'

'No, I'm afraid you'll have to choose between sherry, gin, whisky and brandy.'

'Then sherry, please.' Irene had sat down and was looking round. 'Mum, I like this house. It's just the kind of house I hope I'll be able to afford some day. Do you think people are going to be afraid of it because of the murders that happened here?'

Constance was pouring out sherry for Irene and herself. 'Are you hoping that that might bring the price down to something within your reach?'

'Now who's being absurd?' Irene said. 'Why are you being so bitchy to me, Mum?'

'I'm sorry, I'm sorry, I'm really sorry, darling.' Constance dropped into a chair, facing Irene. 'After all the things that have been happening, I don't think I'm quite myself. Tell me about this man you're thinking of marrying.'

'His name's Samuel. And he's teaching me to play the French horn. And he's got a job with a small publishing firm who publish mostly very technical things about archæology. He's really very learned. I know you'll like him. And he's fifty-two.'

'But that's more than twenty years older than you!' Constance exclaimed.

'What's wrong with that? He's very youthful in his outlook and I think I'm rather mature in mine.'

This was something that Constance had never noticed, but she did not dispute it.

'You may be right,' she said, falling back on her usual formula for avoiding an argument. 'Has he any name besides Samuel?'

'Yes, it's Blythe. And I think that's a very nice name, because he's really such a blithe person.'

'I'm glad you like it. My trouble is I can't get used to this habit that's got around of calling people by their first names, and probably kissing them too, the first time you meet them. It's my generation.' Constance had begun to think that marrying someone twenty years older than herself might be just what Irene needed. 'Am I going to meet him?'

'Of course. I'd have brought him down here today if he hadn't been getting settled into my flat.'

'How long are you staying?'

'That rather depends on how long you need me. They've been very understanding at the shop. Naturally there was no problem about my coming today, as it's Sunday, but when I phoned my boss this morning to tell him what had happened, he told me I needn't hurry back. He just wants me to phone him this evening to tell him what the position is.'

So that he could question Irene closely, get an inside story about the murders and write it up quickly to sell to some newspaper, Constance thought. Then she began to wonder what was happening to her. Why was she having such shocking thoughts about everybody? Had she always been like that, she wondered. Had a sceptical attitude, a lack of sympathy, a tendency to mockery on her part, really been to blame for most of Irene's eccentricities? She was a dear girl, really. Had not the speed with which she had come to Long Meldon demonstrated that? Constance hoped very much that she was going to like Samuel.

The front doorbell rang.

Irene jerked upright in her chair. 'Who's that? Is it the police?'

'I should think that's unlikely,' Constance said. 'They've been here already this morning.'

She went to the front door and opened it. Pauling stood there.

'I'm glad you're still here,' he said. 'I wasn't sure you would be.'

'I'm leaving soon,' she said. 'But come in.' He stepped inside and she closed the door. 'Have the police been to see you this morning?'

'Yes, that's why I came,' he said. 'I wanted to find out if you can make any more sense of things than I can. After all, we were together for some of yesterday morning, weren't we? Have you told them that?'

'Oh yes.' She was leading him towards the dining-room. 'This is my daughter, Irene. This is Mr Pauling, the husband of Margot, who was shot by Colin.'

'Hallo,' Irene said rather lugubriously. His arrival did not seem to exhilarate her.

'Hallo,' Pauling replied in an equally muted tone.

After that there was a silence. Then Constance remembered to offer Pauling a drink and he asked for whisky. But though he had appeared ready, indeed eager, to talk when he first saw Constance, the presence of Irene seemed to have discouraged him. He looked as if he did not know what he was doing there.

'Irene got here only a few minutes ago,' Constance said, feeling that the two must be explained to one another. 'She heard about the shooting on the seven o'clock news and she knew that I was working here, so she came straight down. But she doesn't really know much about what's happened.'

'Does she know about this unfortunate girl, Jennifer?' Pauling asked.

'Come to think of it, I don't suppose she does,' Constance said. 'Irene, there seems to have been a murder that the Press haven't got hold of yet. A girl called Jennifer Hyland who's been running a café in the village for some time made a cake for Colin's birthday, which should have been today, and she brought it up here yesterday morning and left it on the kitchen table. And then she disappeared. Her sister got very worried about her not coming home and got in touch with the police about it and this morning they found the girl drowned in a pool near here. Only before drowning she'd been hit hard on the head with what the police are inclined to think may have been the poker from the drawing-room fireplace here. In other words, she was probably knocked unconscious here and carried out to her car and driven up to this pool where they found her, all because she saw something which was very dangerous to somebody.'

'So you mean Colin didn't murder all those people?' Irene said.

'Perhaps not all,' Constance answered. 'What I thought Inspector Frayne believed was that someone came in and found what Colin had done or was just doing, and as there was a gun lying there handy he decided to grab it and add another death to the count. And Jennifer saw that and so was killed and taken away and dumped in the pool.'

'And that's absurd, you know,' Pauling said. 'It doesn't take one very serious thing into account.'

Constance turned her head to look at him questioningly. He did not meet her gaze because he was looking intently at Irene, who was returning his stare with an expression of uncertainty which was not characteristic of her. She usually knew what she thought on most matters.

'Why is it absurd?' Constance asked.

'Because whoever did it had to get away from the pool, as well as to it,' Pauling said. 'All right, suppose Jennifer walked in on the scene here and saw someone take the gun that had fallen out of Colin's hand and shoot someone with it—Margot, the police are obviously fairly sure—and suppose Jennifer made a scene, even tried to stop it, perhaps tried to ring 999, and so was hit on the head and knocked unconscious, then bundled into her own car, driven up to the pool and pushed into it—then whoever did that had to

get away. And he had to walk. If he'd driven Jennifer to the
pool in her car, as I understand he did, he can't have driven
away from there in his own. So he had to walk back into
Long Meldon, if that was where he came from, and take up
his normal life as if he'd never been away. And that would
have taken a bit of doing. So in my view the police idea is
absurd. I think the girl gave some hitch-hiker a lift in the
lane and when he'd murdered her he simply walked on
along it, I don't know in which direction, and by now he's
God knows where.'

'Tell me,' Irene said, still eyeing him in her unusually
dubious way, 'have you ever been in Long Meldon before?'

'Not for around fifteen or sixteen years,' he answered. 'I
live in Sydney.'

'Ah, but you have been here long ago,' she said.

'I think so, yes. I'm fairly sure of it, though I can't
remember much about it. I used to live in Bracklington and
I'd a liking for walking in those days and I probably
came here sometime on one of my rambles, though I've an
impression it's all very much changed. I don't seem to
recognize any of it.'

'But the pool wouldn't have changed, would it?'

'Perhaps not. No, I imagine it wouldn't. Why?'

'Only that if you'd never been here before, I mean literally
never, you couldn't possibly have known there was any pool
where there is one. I know it, you know. I used to live in
Bracklington myself and I did a bit of rambling too, and I
remember once some friends and I sat down by that pool
and ate our lunches there.'

A look of astonished anger appeared on Pauling's face.

'You're implying I could have been the person who took
the girl up to it and drowned her!' he exclaimed.

'No,' Irene said mildly, 'I was trying to clear you. I
thought if you didn't know these parts at all you couldn't
possibly know where to find a pool to drown her in. But you
did know about it, so I can't help you, that's all I meant.'

'Only how did I get back to the Green Dragon without being noticed?' There was a mocking look on his face now, as if he had decided that she need not be taken seriously. 'I still believe in the hitch-hiker.'

'Perhaps someone did notice you,' Irene said. 'You can't yet be sure they didn't, can you?'

'No doubt the police will find out about that fairly soon. I'll either be under arrest by the evening or else on my way back to Sydney. But if you don't like my theory about the hitch-hiker . . .' He paused.

'Yes?' Constance said.

He looked back at her. His anger seemed only to have been momentary. His face now was sad and tired.

'No,' he said, 'think it out for yourself. Logically there's really only one person who could have done it. I mean, who could have got away from the pool without being noticed. But I'm not going to start making trouble when after all I could be wrong. Mrs Lawley, to go back to what I said when I came here, you and I had coffee together yesterday morning and we saw Jennifer Hyland leaving in her car, you thought to bring the birthday cake here. But the police seem to be sure she didn't come here straight away and want to know where she spent the short time they can't account for. Have you any ideas about it?'

She shook her head. 'None at all. My guess is, it isn't important. But I think I understand what you mean when you say there's only one person who could have got away from the pool without any risk of being noticed. You mean Conrad Greer, don't you? I believe the pool is only a little way up the lane beyond his house. So all he had to do, if he killed Jennifer, was walk straight home. He might have had bad luck and been seen by someone in the lane, but I've noticed that very few people come along it, on foot or by car. And if your wife was his victim he had a possible motive for getting rid of her, hadn't he?'

'For getting rid of Margot? *He* had?' But though his tone

was incredulous, it seemed to Constance that his eyes were wary. 'You don't mean because she broke off with him all those years ago?'

'I wasn't actually thinking of that,' she said.

'And you don't mean he may have got the idea that she was going to take Colin away from him. If anyone thought that, they didn't know Margot. The last thing she ever wanted was to be burdened with a child.'

'Let's leave it at that,' she said. 'As you said yourself just now, I could be wrong and I don't want to start making trouble for an innocent person.'

'So you're very sure of yourself, aren't you, but for some reason you're afraid of saying so?' His tone had suddenly become hostile. 'Then we'll none of us say what we think. I'd better be going. Goodbye. Goodbye, Irene.'

She did not answer, but sat looking thoughtfully after him as Constance saw him to the front door.

When she came back, Irene said, 'Of course you realize he's the murderer, don't you?'

'What on earth makes you say that?' Constance asked.

'Oh, it's just something one knows,' Irene said. 'I knew it as soon as I saw him. You've always known I was very intuitive, haven't you? And during this last year or two in the community I've been specially training myself. I could tell at once. Besides that, you're afraid of him.'

This was a little nearer to the truth than Constance had expected. In the last few minutes, without understanding it, she had felt a sense of fear of the man building up in her. Doing her best to rationalize it, she said, 'There's a possibility that he and Conrad Greer were involved together in something pretty crooked. And if they were and Margot knew about it, or was even involved in it herself, and if she threatened Greer after she got home that she might be going to give him away if he didn't pay her blackmail, then he would have had a motive for killing her. But that applies to Pauling too, only, as he pointed out, it's unlikely he could

have got all the way back to the Green Dragon from the
pool without anyone noticing him, whereas Greer had only
a short walk back to his house.'

'Mum, darling, you really are too simple,' Irene said and
as Constance sat down again at the table she reached out
and patted her hand affectionately. 'You're saying precisely
what he wanted you to say. It's why he came here. It was
to put that idea into your head so that you'd suggest it to
the police, instead of his having to do it himself. It would
be so much more subtle and convincing, coming from you,
than from him. But the obvious fact is he simply walked
back into the village after leaving the poor girl in the pool
and just had the sort of good luck that people like him often
have of not meeting anybody. If he had met somebody, he'd
probably have said what a nice day it was and what a
pleasant walk he'd been having. But he knew he hadn't met
anybody, so he knew he was quite safe to say what he did
to you. But what's this crooked thing he and Conrad Greer
are supposed to have been involved in and that it frightened
you to mention to him?'

Constance did not answer at once. She had not made
up her mind how far to confide in Irene. Then she said
uncertainly, 'For all I know, there may be no truth in it
whatever. That's why I didn't want to talk about it. But
the police seem to think that Conrad Greer's been a receiver
of stolen property for some time and his shop in Bracklington
is just a front for his other activities. They've been keeping
an eye on him recently and it seems he's been shipping stuff
off to the Paulings in Australia, though whether they knew
it was stolen isn't quite clear. I think they did, but I don't
think it's certain, any more than it's absolutely sure that
Greer's really a fence. He had some stolen chessmen in his
possession yesterday, but he may not have known they were
stolen. He was going to give them as a birthday present to
Colin, because chess was the strongest passion in his life,
and Greer brought them here a few hours after the murders

and Inspector Frayne found them and pounced on them and took them away. And apparently it's definite that they were stolen, but if Greer had known that, would he have brought them here when the place was crawling with police?'

'Of course he would have,' Irene said. 'If you've a certain sort of criminal mind you believe you can get away with anything. Or he might actually have brought them here on purpose to induce you to think just what you do, that he'd never have taken the risk of bringing them if he'd known they were stolen. Again, it'll be much more subtle and convincing if it's you who suggests that to the police than if he has to do it. Oh, Mum dear, it's really time I came down to look after you, isn't it? You've got such a nice innocent mind. Meanwhile, d'you know what I'd like?' .

'Some lunch?'

'Oh yes, some lunch, of course. But I'd very much like to meet this Conrad Greer. I remember his shop in Brackling-ton, but I've never been into it. Could we get him here on some pretext or other? Or could we call on him?'

The thought of getting lunch was comforting to Constance. It was normal, it was rational, it was something that she knew how to do. She finished her sherry and stood up.

'Are you beginning to have doubts about your instant diagnosis of Kenneth Pauling as a murderer?' she asked.

'Good Lord no, that's as clear as day,' Irene answered. 'But I'm very interested in the criminal mind. In people, I mean, who truly reject the dictates of society. I'd really like to meet Conrad Greer.'

CHAPTER 7

Constance did not want to meet Conrad Greer. She did not want to meet anybody. She wished she were at home, sitting down by herself to eat a ham sandwich or perhaps some beans on toast, with no one, not even Irene, to intrude on her peaceful privacy. But Irene was here and ready to eat some lunch even if after it she would be anxious to proceed with some detective work. For that was what it was, Constance thought, that Irene really wanted to do. She might have claimed that by sheer instinct she had already spotted the murderer, but it would please her, would make her feel that she was pandering successfully to the prejudices of people more commonplace than herself, if she could collect some evidence against him.

Meanwhile, there was lunch. Thank heaven for lunch, Constance thought. Shopping in the village the day before she had bought some garlic pâté which was in the refrigerator. Putting it out on plates for Irene and herself, she made some toast and some coffee, then called to Irene to come and eat in the kitchen. Irene strolled in, looking deeply abstracted, lost in thoughts which no doubt she felt that this was not the right time to express. She settled down to spreading pâté on her toast, either munching dreamily or gazing out of the window.

She had finished toast and pâté and was leaning her elbows on the table, holding her cup of coffee in both hands, when she said, 'All right, you don't want us to call on Greer, but what do you want to do? Are we going to stay here till they've solved the crime?'

'You needn't stay at all, you know,' Constance said. 'It was your idea to come.'

'And a good thing I did, as I said. You'll swallow anything anyone tells you without even trying to see what's behind it. That's as long as it isn't me that tells you. You never believe anything I say.'

'Oh, it surely isn't as bad as that,' Constance said. 'You aren't a liar, it's just that you let your fantasies run away with you.'

'You mean I con myself before I start trying to con other people.'

'That's a rather unkind way of putting it.'

'But it's what you think.'

Constance was a little surprised that Irene should have gone so far in self-analysis. She began to wonder what sort of man Samuel was. Had his influence had something to do with it?

'It's just that what I've got to do this afternoon is to go to the police station in Bracklington and make a full statement about finding the bodies and so on,' she said. 'You can come with me or not, as you like.'

'And after that you mean to go home?'

'It's what I'd like to do unless there's some very good reason for staying here.'

'Very well, let's go home. You've had a bad time here. I can understand you want to get away. But perhaps we could look in on Greer in the morning. I mean, he'll be back in his shop, won't he? We could go in and perhaps even buy something, a pretty snuff-box or something. We could tell him I'm getting married and that you're looking for a wedding present for me, then our going in wouldn't look suspicious.'

'I can't think of anything that would look more suspicious,' Constance said. 'If you really want to go in to see him we'll tell him we want to talk to him about the murders and find out what he thinks. That strikes me as a fairly normal thing to do.'

'All right, if that's how you want to handle it. Now what about getting along to that police station you've got to go to?'

Constance stood up and automatically started to put the plates and cups that they had used into the dishwasher when she realized that she would not be here to run it later, so she washed them under the tap and was in the act of putting them away in the cupboard from which she had taken them when the doorbell rang yet again.

'That'll be the police, won't it?' Irene said.

'I don't know,' Constance replied.

'Are you expecting anyone else?'

'No.'

'Well, you won't tell them what I said about the Pauling man, will you? That's something just between you and me.'

'I wouldn't dream of it.'

'It would be all right if we had some of the sort of evidence that would convince people like them, but I know how they can sneer and try to make you feel a fool if they don't understand you.'

The bell rang again. Constance hurried out into the hall and opened the door.

A man whom she had never seen before stood there. He was a small man in a neat grey suit and a grey and white striped shirt with a sober, dark blue tie. He was about forty, had a long, smooth-featured face and sandy hair neatly parted on one side, a smile that looked politely diffident but did not reach his small grey eyes, which regarded Constance with what struck her as a coolly observant manner. She wondered for a moment if he was a plain clothes detective, but thought that he was too small ever to have been accepted into the police force.

'Mrs Lawley?' he asked.

'Yes,' she said.

'I believe you're the caretaker here.'

'The housekeeper. And I'm leaving shortly.'

'Ah, I'm sorry I got it wrong,' he said. 'I must have misunderstood Mr Frayne. My name is Collis.' He brought a card out of his pocket and handed it to her. 'I belong to the firm of Stevenson, Bartholomew and Collis. We've acted for some time as Colonel Barrow's solicitors. Mr Frayne chased me down in my home. Being Sunday, no one was in the office, but he was very anxious that one of us should come out here immediately to catch you before you left so that we could make arrangements for a valuer to come in —probate, you know—and for me to take possession of any

obvious valuables such as jewellery, silver and so on, to put
them in our strong-room. Naturally you'll want to verify
my credentials, so please ring up Mr Frayne and ask him if
I'm to be trusted.'

He had spoken rapidly and earnestly, but ended with a
sudden little nervous explosion of laughter, as if there were
something very amusing to him about the idea that anyone
could doubt the integrity of a member of the firm of Stevenson, Bartholomew and Collis.

The name was familiar to Constance as that of one of the
leading firms of solicitors in Bracklington. The only matter
in doubt was whether this man was indeed their Mr Collis.

'I think I ought to do that,' she said.

'Please do, please do. Only proper. I would be much
happier if you'd do that.'

He laughed again, and glad to contribute to his happiness,
Constance picked up the telephone and dialled the police
station in Bracklington.

While she was speaking to Inspector Frayne and being
told that Mr Mortimer Collis was to be expected to call on
her that afternoon and that he was entirely to be trusted,
the man stayed outside on the doorstep as if to make it clear
that he was not the kind of man who might rush in, slam
the door behind him and do damage of some kind to a
defenceless woman. When she had put the telephone down
again she invited him to come in. Irene, meanwhile, had
come to the doorway of the kitchen to find out what was
going on and Constance introduced her and the man to one
another. Then she took him into the dining-room and Irene
followed.

'This is without doubt the most shocking event in my
experience,' he said as they all sat down at the table, 'and
I have been with the firm for nearly twenty years. Of course,
I never was happy about that poor boy. I call him a poor
boy although I suppose he was really a young monster. But
it wasn't his fault. I can't persuade myself it was really his

fault. If he had been born without the normal complement of arms and legs we'd all be sorry for him, but what he was born without was a moral sense, and we can't forgive that.'

Irene murmured, 'The fault, dear Brutus, is not in our stars, but in our genes.'

'I beg your pardon?' he said.

'Nothing,' she said. 'All the same, if you haven't got arms and legs, you can't start killing people, even if you'd like to. But basically I'm sure you're right, he was a poor boy. I'm very sorry for him.'

'If he'd lived,' Constance said, 'who would have taken care of him?'

'I'm not sure,' the man answered. 'It would have been primarily a case for the police.'

'No, I meant if none of the tragedy had happened,' she said. 'The Barrows were both around eighty. Probably neither of them would have lived much longer, or even if they had they wouldn't have been capable of looking after a very difficult adolescent. Do you know if they'd made any provision for that?'

'As a matter of fact, I do, but . . .' He paused, evidently considering whether or not this was something too confidential for him to talk about. 'Well, I don't see why I shouldn't tell you, if you're interested,' he went on. 'I've told the police. Colonel Barrow has made provision for the eventuality you mentioned. My firm were to be responsible for the boy. Mr Stevenson, our senior partner, was to be his guardian.'

'But they'd provided for him, had they?' Irene said. 'I mean, they'd left their money to him.'

Constance felt that the question should not have been asked. She assumed that the contents of the Barrows' wills was confidential, at least for the moment. After their funerals, perhaps, or after the inquests, it would become a matter of public knowledge, but at present this small, precise man would have no right to disclose it. She did not know that lawyers often take the obligation of confidentiality somewhat less seriously than is expected of them.

'It happens to be a rather interesting case,' he said. 'The Barrows left all they possessed to their grandson. But in the event of his predeceasing them, then their estate was to pass to their daughter, Mrs Pauling. And at the moment, you see, there seems to be some degree of uncertainty which died first, the mother or the son. If he shot his mother, as it was at first assumed he had, then he, of course, survived her and stood to inherit the Barrows' money. But if in fact he had killed himself before someone else came in and killed Mrs Pauling, then she probably survived the boy and was their heir.'

'But can you inherit money as the result of committing a crime?' Constance asked. 'I thought you couldn't.'

'Ah, there's that to be considered, of course,' the solicitor said. 'I'm not sure, however, what the position is when the heir is a minor and mentally not entirely responsible for his actions. It's a very interesting question. But in the end, in this case, it happens not to make much difference. The boy himself of course had made no will, so anything he might have inherited would have passed to his next of kin, his mother, and she, we believe, though this has yet to be confirmed, made a will leaving all she had to her husband. So whether the Barrow money came directly to her, or only after it had belonged briefly to her son, it will in any case end up in the possession of Mr Pauling. He happens, as perhaps you know, to be in Long Meldon at the moment, which is very convenient. There's the matter of tax to be considered, of course. It will come to a considerably larger amount if it turns out that the boy was capable of inheriting his grandparents' estate, as there would be two lots of death duties, but it may well be that it isn't possible. However, that brings me to what I really came for this afternoon. I hadn't realized that you intended to leave the house,

Mrs Lawley, and I wanted to arrange with you when it would be convenient for you to let Mr Grigson, the valuer we usually employ on these occasions, to come and make an estimate of the contents of the house so that we can proceed with calculating the tax that will be due. And then there's the matter of removing any outstanding valuables to safe-keeping in our strong-room. Perhaps you can help us there.'

'I don't know anything about that,' Constance said. 'I'm sure you won't feel offended, but the fact is I don't like to feel responsible for removing anything, but perhaps you can get someone from the police to go round the house with you. And the same with your Mr Grigson. My daughter and I are leaving for our home in Bracklington this afternoon, but the police, of course, have keys to the house and could show him round.'

'Ah yes, that will plainly be best.' Mr Collis stood up. 'I'll explain the situation to them and no doubt we can arrange something. Meanwhile, thank you for your time. I'll say good day.'

It was Irene who saw him to the door. Coming back after a moment, she gave a cheerful giggle.

'Poor little man, you offended him terribly, suspecting him of being a thief,' she said. 'I don't suppose anything of the sort has ever happened to a member of the firm of Stevenson, Bartholomew and Collis. You should have seen how stiffly he walked to his car, pretending he didn't feel like hitting me.'

'But I didn't suspect him of anything,' Constance said. 'I'm sure he's just what he said he was.'

'But he didn't think you did.'

'Well, I'm sorry. I'm sure he's just as respectable as he looks, but I could hardly let someone I'd never met before walk off with Mrs Barrow's jewellery, if she has any. I don't know anything about that. Now I suppose we'll have to wait till Mr Collis comes back with a policeman. I do see

that valuables shouldn't be left lying around in an empty
house.'

'It's interesting, isn't it, that Pauling's going to inherit
everything from the Barrows?' Irene said. 'I knew he was
the murderer of his wife, but I thought it was out of rage at
her leaving him. It hadn't occurred to me he'd a good sordid
financial motive as well.'

'He told me about that motive himself,' Constance said.
'I don't think it has anything to do with the murders.'

'And why did he tell you about the motive? Wasn't it
simply to seem to be awfully straightforward and honest to
lull your suspicions? Darling, you are so easy to fool. But
have we really got to wait for the police now?'

'I think we'd better.'

As it turned out, they did not have to wait very long. In
less than an hour Mr Collis returned, accompanied, to
Constance's surprise, by three constables. It seemed an
unnecessarily large force to send for the protection of the
Barrows' silver and jewellery. But only one of these policemen remained in the house with the solicitor, going from
room to room, opening doors and cupboards and from
time to time extracting some object which apparently they
considered valuable. The other two men remained in the
garden, poking about among flowers and shrubs, appearing
to be searching for something.

Irene seemed to have been right that Constance had
offended Mr Collis, for he was far less friendly now than he
had been during his first visit. But she and Irene did not
stay to see his work completed. Constance at last finished
packing her suitcase, Irene collected her own case and her
French horn, and the two of them set off for Bracklington
in the Mini.

Constance felt a sense of intense relief when they left Long
Meldon behind them. Not only Riverside, but the whole
village, seemed pervaded with horror. Passing Jenny's Café
she saw that curtains were drawn across the windows and

that a notice hung on the door, saying, 'Closed'. They passed the Green Dragon where she supposed Kenneth Pauling was still staying. It was unlikely that he would leave before his wife's funeral, at the earliest, and if in fact he stood to inherit all that the Barrows had had to leave, then he would probably want a chance to consult their solicitors before leaving for Australia. If he was able to leave. Might he not have to stay here? For the first time since Irene had proclaimed her certainty of his guilt, Constance found herself wondering if her daughter might not have more wisdom than she had ever given her credit for.

The afternoon was bright, the sunshine glittering on the road ahead of them and on the vivid green of meadows to left and right of it. When they drove into Bracklington Constance drove first to the police station. There she asked for Inspector Frayne, but it was the monosyllabic Sergeant Randall, who had accompanied Frayne on his first visit to Riverside, who took her statement, gave it to her to sign, thanked her and would have ushered them out to the car if Irene had not checked him with a question.

'Those men who are out at Riverside with Mr Collis, sergeant,' she said, 'I suppose they're looking for the weapon that was used to brain Jennifer Hyland, aren't they?'

He had one of the blankest faces that Constance had ever seen. It showed no trace of expression as he answered, 'I couldn't say, Miss Lawley.'

'But of course you could,' Irene said. 'It's just that you think you shouldn't.'

'Come along, Irene,' Constance said. 'We don't want to waste the sergeant's time.'

'Only I can't see why he shouldn't tell us that,' Irene said. 'They're looking for that poker, aren't they, Sergeant?'

He merely gazed at her without making any answer at all, while Constance, grasping Irene by the arm, succeeded in steering her out to the Mini.

They spent the evening watching television, except for a short interruption in it when Irene telephoned Samuel. She did it while Constance was cooking a meal for them, or rather, heating up a steak and kidney pie from Marks & Spencer that she had in the freezer and boiling some potatoes and some frozen spinach to go with it. Living alone, as she had been doing for the last few years, she had grown to rely more and more on take-away foods which she need not trouble to cook for herself. But oddly enough, one of the attractions of the kind of job to which she was sent by the Bracklington Helpers was that it made demands on her culinary abilities. The kind of people for whom she worked naturally expected her to provide good food for them and she always felt more pleasure than she would ever have expected of herself, in the days when she had cooked for a family and had sometimes felt very tired of it, in cooking with care and interest and being praised for it.

She went to bed early, far more tired than she normally was when she returned home from a job, and was asleep before Irene went to her room.

In the morning Constance was wakened by a strange sound. At first it seemed to her to be part of a dream in which she was still lost, and burying her head in her pillow she tried to emerge from her drowsiness and to escape from the noise. But it was not a dream. It was Irene, practising the French horn. The fact penetrated suddenly to Constance's consciousness and she recognized abruptly that in fact she was wide awake.

She sat up in bed. Until now she had been congratulating herself on the fact that Irene had given up her chanting and so the sound of it would not be inflicted on her, but this was more penetrating, more overpowering than the chanting had ever been. She wondered if Samuel really believed that Irene could be taught to play the thing properly, or whether, once they were married, he would bring her round tactfully to recognizing that music was not her strong point, and that something quiet, like painting watercolours, might be a more rewarding form of self-expression for her.

Getting up and putting on her dressing-gown, Constance went to the door of Irene's room, put her head into it and shouted, 'Breakfast in ten minutes!'

She was not sure if Irene heard her, but she went downstairs and proceeded to make coffee and toast.

She had reached her second cup of coffee when Irene appeared, also in a dressing-gown, and sitting down at the kitchen table, where Constance ate most of her meals when she was at home, helped herself to coffee and toast and marmalade.

'I've been thinking,' Irene announced. It was an activity for which Constance had often felt her daughter was not too well fitted, but she waited for her to go on. 'We agreed yesterday, didn't we, that we'd look in on the Greer shop this morning?'

'I suppose we did,' Constance said reluctantly.

'You don't want to do it now?' Irene asked.

'Not particularly. I'd like to have a very quiet day and among other things ring the Helpers and find out if I am going to be paid anything for the time I put in at Long Meldon. I was taken on for a week, but I only stayed four days and they were a bit peculiar, so perhaps I ought not to expect to be paid at all.'

'Now that's just like you!' Irene exclaimed. 'Of course they must pay you for the whole week. It wasn't your fault that things got peculiar.'

'I certainly hope not.'

'Have you a contract of employment? Have you a clause written into it that in the event you have to return home early because of circumstances beyond your control, you have to forfeit any of the amount that would normally have been due to you for doing the full time?'

'Good heavens no! It's never anything as formal as that.

Mrs Jay at the Helpers rings me up and asks me if I'm free
to take on a job, and she tells me a little about it and I get
in my car and tootle along to it. But what's happened to
you, Irene? You always said one shouldn't think about
money. You disdained it.'

'Well, I've changed, that's all,' Irene said. 'I like it.'

'I'm so glad to hear it. Not that one should think too
much about it if one's fortunate enough not to be compelled
to do so, but I think it's a healthy sign to take a reasonable
interest in it.'

'Mum, you aren't *short* of money, are you?' Irene asked.
'I mean, you take on the sort of job you do because you
want an interest in life, not because you couldn't get by
financially without it? Because if that's how it is, I'm sure
Samuel and I could help you.'

Constance had never in her life expected to hear such
words from Irene. She was beginning to feel that she had
somehow badly misunderstood her daughter.

'That's very sweet of you and I do appreciate it,' she said,
'but you're quite right, I take on these jobs because normally
I enjoy them, though of course the pay is welcome. I don't
suppose I could have afforded to go to Madeira last year if
I hadn't been earning. But I don't think your Samuel should
have to finance my luxuries. I'm hoping he won't regard
having a mother-in-law as a burden. But we were talking
about going to the Greer shop this morning. I don't mind
going if that's what you want to do, but are you sure it's
wise?'

'Why shouldn't it be?'

'Only that we're bound to find ourselves getting more
and more involved with these murders, when it would
obviously be best to leave them to the police.'

'Why obviously?'

'Well, it's their job, isn't it? We'll only get under their
feet.'

'They always used to be supposed to have such big feet,

didn't they? One doesn't seem to hear so much about that
any more.' Irene reached for a second slice of toast. 'But I'd
like to meet the man, you know. I'd like to be able to trust
my own intuitions. Suppose when I meet him I feel quite
certain that he's the murderer and that my certainty about
Pauling was wrong, that would be very interesting scientifi-
cally. It isn't always one has the opportunity of making an
experiment like that. But if you don't want to come I could
go by myself.'

The thought of letting Irene loose in the Greer shop,
making whatever form of experiment happened to appeal
to her imagination, filled Constance with consternation.
Hastily she said, 'No, it's all right, I'll come. And if you like
we'll look for a wedding present for you. You must tell me
if you see something you like.'

'Yesterday you said that would look very suspicious,'
Irene said. 'You said we ought simply to talk straight away
about the murders.'

'Yes, it's what I think we ought to do, but if it's a case of
really buying you a present I don't see why we shouldn't
do it, though I suppose when it comes to the point I
ought to supply you with sheets and towels, or perhaps
cooking-pots or a dishwasher or something.'

'Please, please!' Irene cried. 'Let's look for something nice
at Greer's. Samuel and I haven't the least idea how we
mean to live. We might live in a caravan, or somewhere
there isn't any electricity, or go prowling around Europe for
a while on bicycles, or even on foot. I'll tell you when we
need the sheets and towels. But now let's go along to
Greer's.'

She stood up and started to clear the table.

They were both dressed and ready to leave for their visit
to Conrad Greer's shop when they were checked by the
arrival of a visitor.

For a moment Constance could not think who the woman
was who stood on the doorstep, though she knew that she

had seen her before. It was the scarf over her head that did it, nearly hiding her carefully arranged grey curls. She was a tall, sombre-faced woman of about fifty and when Constance had seen her last, as she quickly remembered, she had been in trousers and a shirt, not in the neat light blue suit that she was wearing now. She was Mrs Newcome, who had cleaned Riverside for the Barrows.

'Good morning, Mrs Lawley,' she said. 'I hope I haven't come at an inconvenient time.'

'Oh no, come in,' Constance said, though she could not think why the woman should want to see her, unless it was simply to gossip about the tragedy at Riverside. She took her into the sitting-room and introduced her to Irene.

'Good morning,' Mrs Newcome said. 'I'm glad to see you here. Your mother must need some support after what she's been through. Mrs Lawley—' she turned to Constance— 'I'd be grateful for some advice, but not if I'm intruding. The fact is, this morning was one of my usual mornings for Riverside, but as I'm not wanted there now I thought I'd come into town and have my hair done and do a bit of shopping, and then I thought: Well, perhaps Mrs Lawley could tell me if I ought to go to the police, or if I'm worrying about nothing. I don't want to go to the police. Once you get mixed up with them, you don't know where you may end up, perhaps having to be a witness in a court or something. But I want to do my duty.'

They had all sat down in the small, bright room that overlooked a small garden in which there were still a few roses in bloom, though they were past their summer prime and the September blooming had not yet begun.

'I'm sure you do,' Constance said, 'though I'd be surprised if there's anything useful in any advice I can give you.'

Mrs Newcome clasped her hands around the bulging plastic handbag that she was carrying.

'Some of it I've already told the police,' she said. 'They

came round asking questions and they told me they wanted to know if I'd seen Miss Hyland any time on Saturday morning. Well, I had, as I told them. I saw her just after she'd driven away from the café and I waved to her and she came into my house and had a cup of coffee with me. I don't know why, but the police seemed very interested in that. She was only with me about twenty minutes or thereabouts. I didn't see why it should be important.'

'I think I understand why it is,' Constance said. 'They've been worried, you see, because they think she was murdered only just before I got back to Riverside, yet if she'd gone straight there after I saw her leave the café, she must have been in the house some time. And that upset all their ideas of how the murders happened. But if she spent some time with you, there's no problem about that.'

'Those murders!' Mrs Newcome said. 'Well, I think I told you I'd seen him shriek and storm, didn't I, and that I was always very careful with him myself, but I never dreamt it would come to murder. Trouble of some sort wouldn't have surprised me, but murder! He could be a nice lad too in between whiles, so I sort of got attached to him. But I suppose finding out the truth about his mother was just too much for someone like him. I don't understand why he killed his grandparents, though. They'd been very good to him.'

'He seems to have been furious with them because of the lies they'd told him,' Constance said, 'and I believe in his place I'd have been furious too. It would have been far better for him to have had to face the truth from the beginning.'

'Trial by fury,' Irene observed. 'He tried them in his own mind for perjury and found them guilty.'

'But it isn't about that cup of coffee you gave Miss Hyland that you want my advice, is it?' Constance said. 'You say you've already told the police about that.'

'No, it isn't about that,' Mrs Newcome said. 'The trouble

is, I'm maybe just being silly, thinking about something that doesn't mean anything. If I'd thought of telling the police about it when they were in my house it would have seemed natural, so to speak, and they might have been interested, or they might not, it wouldn't have been my responsibility. But I don't want them thinking I'm the sort of person who pokes her nose into things just for the thrill of it. Honestly, I'm not like that, Mrs Lawley.'

'I'm sure you're not, Mrs Newcome,' Constance said.

'I did feel tempted to just ring them up and tell them the facts and ring off—you know what I mean, one of those anonymous phone calls one hears the police are always getting. But I knew I wouldn't respect myself if I did that. So then I thought I wouldn't do anything about it. But then I suddenly thought, as I was coming into Bracklington to get my hair done, I'd just look in on you and see if you think I ought to go to the police after all.'

By now Constance was feeling that whatever the information was of which Mrs Newcome was in possession it should most certainly be given to the police. The build-up that she had given it made it seem sure that it was important.

'Well, what's your problem?' Constance asked.

'It's just that I saw Mr Greer in the village in the afternoon,' Mrs Newcome replied. She said it almost in a whisper, as if she were not sure that she wanted even Irene to overhear her. 'He drove up to the café and went in and in a minute he came out again. I saw him because I was just going into the grocer's. And when I came out the car was gone, but a funny thing was . . .' She hesitated, frowning as if she found some difficulty in following her own line of thought. 'There's a card they hang on the door, saying "Open" or "Closed", depending which way round they hang it. But I'm sure it said "Open" when I went into the grocer's, as it always was on a Saturday afternoon, that's when the best trade was, but when I came out it said "Closed".'

'I see,' Constance said. She did not exactly see, but she began to have a feeling that what she had been told might indeed be important. 'We know now, of course, that Jennifer Hyland wasn't there to run things in the normal way, but isn't there a woman who works there, a small woman who wears a pink overall? If she was there she could have kept things going, couldn't she?'

'Mrs Crisp,' Mrs Newcome said. 'She doesn't work on a Saturday afternoon, she and her husband always come in to town to do the weekend shopping. It's cheaper if you come in to the supermarket here than if you stick to the grocer in the village, and Saturday's the only day Mr Crisp's at home to drive the car and can bring her in.'

'What about the other Miss Hyland then—Miss Julie Hyland?' Constance asked. 'Couldn't she have kept the place open?'

Mrs Newcome gave a faint shake of her head. 'She probably wouldn't care to do that. She'd help her sister a bit if she was at home, but she never did care for the work. If Miss Jennifer didn't come home when she was expected, I think Miss Julie might have closed the place.'

'But only after Mr Greer called.'

'That's right.'

'It's rather odd, isn't it?'

'That's what I can't help thinking.'

'Do you know what time it was when you saw him go into the café?'

'Not really. Some time between two and half past, I'd say. I didn't happen to look at my watch.'

'Well, I'd certainly tell the police about it,' Constance said. 'There's probably some quite simple explanation, but anything to do with that café on Saturday might be important.'

Mrs Newcome gave a sigh and stood up.

'I was really hoping you'd tell me I needn't bother about it,' she said, 'but I suppose even if you had I'd have gone

on worrying about it. So it's best for me to get it over and
be done with it. I think I'll go along to the police station
now.'

'My daughter and I are just going out,' Constance said.
'We're taking the car. I could drive you there if that would
help you.'

'That's very kind. Thank you. Yes, it would be a help.'

Mrs Newcome appeared very grateful for the lift, but
her presence in the car prevented Constance and Irene
discussing the information that she had given them, and
after they had left her at the police station they drove
straight to the shop called 'Conrad Greer, Antiques', were
fortunate in finding parking-space near it, and went into
the shop.

It was in an arcade, for pedestrians only. Most of the
other shops in the arcade were antique shops, or sold
china and glassware, or expensive-looking confectionery, or
fabulously costly woollen goods. Conrad Greer's shop was
one of the largest there. It had a window on either side of
its door and as Constance and Irene entered Greer himself,
with the assistance of Julie Hyland, was moving a bow-
fronted chest of drawers into one of the windows. He looked
up at Constance, smiled and said, 'I'll be with you in a
moment.' Then he continued to manœuvre the moderately
massive yet elegant-looking piece of furniture into the exact
place that he wanted for it.

Julie Hyland looked round at them and said, 'Good
morning', then when the chest of drawers had been de-
posited where Greer wanted, she began to wander round
the shop, looking for ornaments to put on top of it to create
an attractive display. She found a flowery soup tureen and
some silver candlesticks which satisfied her and arranged
them carefully while Greer came to greet Constance and
Irene.

Constance introduced Irene. He held out a hand to her,
but withdrew it before she had taken it, saying, 'Sorry, my

hands are dirty. I've just been polishing up that chest. Nice, don't you think? It's Biedermeier. To get a really good price for it I'll have to send it to Germany. They're buying back all they can of their own antiques which they parted with for a song when times were hard for them.'

'So you send some of your things abroad, do you?' Constance said.

His gaze sharpened slightly at the question. 'Oh, they've been telling you about that, have they? I've sent a good deal of stuff to Ken and Margot in Sydney. Does that seem strange to you?'

'It's nothing to do with me,' she answered. She looked round the shop and found a chair on which she thought that it would be safe to sit down.

Irene wandered across the shop to examine the chest of drawers in the window.

'I mean, that the Paulings and I should have been on good enough terms to have business dealings, after what happened in the past,' Greer said. 'You know all about that by now, I assume. That Colin was my son. And you were there when I walked in and found Margot there and you saw that that was quite a shock to me. Not an altogether agreeable shock. It's one thing to be corresponding with people at the other end of the world and receiving the occasional cheque from them, and another to find yourself, without warning, face to face. I imagine if poor Margot had lived we'd be on friendly enough terms by now. Our affair didn't go deep, you know. She was a bit of a nympho, as Pauling no doubt later discovered to his cost. If Colin hadn't arrived, I don't suppose he'd ever have known anything about her and me. Now what else do you want to know?'

His tone was bitter. Constance made an embarrassed gesture with one hand.

'I'm sorry, that isn't what I came to ask you about at all,' she said.

'You don't want to know if I'm a receiver of stolen property?'

She saw the stormy look in his eyes and tried to defend herself against it with a smile.

'Well, are you?' she asked.

For a moment he seemed to be taken aback by the question, then he laughed.

'Forgive me,' he said. 'You're quite right, of course. If I were I shouldn't tell you. But you do know those chessmen I was going to give Colin were stolen, don't you?'

'So Mr Frayne told me.'

'And for all I know, that chair you're sitting on was stolen. I bought a set of six like that at an auction, but I didn't inquire into how they got there. But now tell me, why did you come in here this morning? It wasn't just as a customer, was it?'

Irene had turned back from the window and was standing beside Constance. Before Constance could reply, she said, 'Actually it was. I'm getting married and we're here to choose a wedding-present if we can find something that appeals to us. What's that over there?'

She was pointing at a plate propped up on a shelf. It had a bold floral pattern of an unusual shade of green on a creamy background and was very attractive, Constance thought, though it seemed to her too modest a thing to be an adequate wedding-present.

'It's Marseilles *faïence*,' Greer answered. 'I wasn't sure what it was myself, so I had it identified by Sotheby's.'

'Is it very expensive?' Irene asked.

'To a friend I'd part with it for forty-five pounds,' he said, smiling, 'but you don't want it, do you? You want to know if I murdered poor little Jennifer Hyland.'

'I don't,' Irene said sharply, 'because I know who did. But if you don't want to sell us that plate, you've only to say so.'

'What the hell d'you mean, you know who did it?' he

demanded. The smile had quite gone. 'You're here just out
of curiosity, aren't you? You're drawn by the smell of
murder. It pulls at you and excites you, like a hound on the
trail of a fox. And you'd like to be in at the kill, wouldn't
you? You'd like to get your teeth into the poor bloody beast
and pull it to pieces. People like you make me sick. If you
want that plate, all right, you can have it for nothing. Get
Julie to wrap it up for you and take it away. But I'm going
out now. I've things to do and I don't want to waste my
time on people who don't even honestly say what they really
want with me. Julie, give them the plate.'

With a black scowl on his face, he strode out of the shop.

CHAPTER 8

Irene looked at Julie with an expression of bewilderment on
her face.

'Now what made him explode like that?' she said. 'How
did I upset him?'

Julie gave a curious smile.

'Do you want the plate?' she asked.

'Not like that,' Irene said. 'I mean, we'll buy it for
forty-five pounds, if that's what it's worth, but I don't want
it for nothing. Not like that.'

'You don't seem to know when you're in luck,' Julie said.
She looked at Constance. 'You don't really want anything,
do you?'

'Not really, no,' Constance replied.

'I'm sorry, he's in a very nervous state,' Julie said. 'You
can hardly blame him, can you?'

It seemed to Constance that in view of the fact that Julie's
sister had been murdered only two days ago, she herself was
surprisingly calm. She stood leaning against the Biedermeier chest with her hands in the pockets of the well-fitting

slacks that she was wearing and she met Constance's eyes
with a sardonic glint in her own. Her handsome face was
perhaps a little paler than when Constance had seen her
last and there was a hollowness about her cheeks that had
not been there then, but she seemed tired rather than tense
and did not look in the least likely to explode like her
employer, partner, or whatever he was.

'Has he been much bothered by the police?' Constance
asked.

'A certain amount,' Julie answered, 'but not actually
about the murders. They asked him where he was at the
time Colin started shooting and he hasn't any alibi, and
they know that he and Margot had an affair years ago and
that Colin was their son, but they didn't really seem much
interested in all that. It's the question of whether or not he
knew that some chessmen he was going to give Colin were
stolen that they've really been battering him about. And if
he did know, then did he know perhaps that other things
we've been handling were stolen? In other words, has he
been a receiver of stolen property for heaven knows how
long? Having that happen on top of the murders has been
just a bit too much for him. He really loved that boy, you
know.'

'Haven't the police been at you too about receiving the
stolen property?' Irene asked.

It was the kind of question that Constance could not have
brought herself to ask, but Irene had all too few inhibitions
when her curiosity happened to have been aroused.

Julie's gaze moved from Constance's face to Irene's with
deepening irony in it.

'Indeed yes,' she answered. 'I'm a very suspicious character.'

'Have you ever suspected that Greer was a fence?' Irene
asked.

'Since you ask me, yes, I have sometimes wondered,' Julie
replied, without giving any sign of taking offence at the

question. 'He bought a good deal of stuff from some rather shady characters. But he isn't a suspicious man himself and if they offered him things cheap he'd more probably think they didn't know the value of what they were handling and that it was a bargain for him. And his wanting to give those chessmen to the boy suggests he didn't know they were stolen.'

'Except that criminals nearly always think they can get away with everything, don't they?' Irene said. 'I mean, they'd never take the risks they do if they thought seriously there was much chance of their being caught.'

'Criminals!' Julie gave an abrupt little laugh. 'It's so extraordinary to think of applying the word to Conrad.'

'But don't you think it's possible he might have assumed it was quite safe to give the chessmen to Colin because no one who could know anything about where they came from was ever going to see them?'

Before Julie could answer Constance said quickly, 'But he knew the police were in the house when he brought them in the afternoon.'

Julie was looking thoughtful. She took some time to respond. Then she said, 'I don't really know the answer to that. Did he bring them because he was quite innocent and didn't know they were stolen, or because he took for granted he could get away with it, as your daughter's suggested, even with the police in the house? I've sometimes wondered about . . .' But then she paused and withdrew her gaze from Irene, looking frowningly before her at nothing in particular.

'Yes?' Constance prompted her after a moment.

'Tell me, what did you think of the Barrows?' Julie asked.

It was not a question that Constance had been expecting.

'I thought they were very charming people,' she said. 'Kind and generous.'

'Both of them?'

'Why, yes.'

'Of course, you only knew Mrs Barrow when she was ill.'

'What has that got to do with it?'

'Don't you think people sometimes get quite unlike themselves when they're ill?' Julie said.

Constance was puzzled.

'Yes, I suppose some of them get very crotchety and irritable,' she answered. 'But certainly that didn't happen to Mrs Barrow. She was very undemanding and always very grateful for even little things that were done for her.'

'That's what I mean,' Julie said. 'When she was well she was quite a tartar. But people like that may get frightened when they're ill. They know they're in your power and they aren't used to it and don't really trust you to be kind to them. So they set about propitiating you in every way they can think of, and people who are really very domineering and perhaps downright dangerous in their way become ever so sweet and gentle. Haven't you seen that happen?'

'I may have,' Constance said, 'but I don't understand what you're talking about. Are you implying that poor little Mrs Barrow could be dangerous to anyone?'

Julie withdrew a hand from her pocket and with one finger began tracing the marquetry pattern on the top of the Biedermeier chest. She looked down, still frowning, at what she was doing as if it needed care.

'I'll tell you an odd thing that used to happen,' she said. 'Perhaps I ought not to say anything about it, but I know you've got involved in the whole thing just by being on the spot, so I don't see why I shouldn't talk to you. From time to time, you see, Mrs Barrow used to come into the shop with Colin. When that happened Conrad would nearly always send me out of the shop with Colin and I'd take him along to the confectioner in the arcade and buy him sweets or something. And it was a bit difficult, because he didn't like me and he'd be horribly sullen the whole time. Then when we got back here Mrs Barrow would be just ready to leave and would be smiling and cheerful and so grateful for the sweets I'd bought for Colin and would tell him to thank me nicely and so on. But the moment she and Colin had gone Conrad would show that he was in a foul temper and would snap my head off and probably rush out of the shop, just as he did this morning, and go to the pub round the corner and start sinking whiskies till he was hardly fit to work for the rest of the day. And once I heard him utter, "I'm going to kill that woman!"' She broke off and gave a deep sigh. 'There, I know I oughtn't to have started telling you about this. You'll think I'm trying to suggest it was the murder of Mrs Barrow that Jennifer saw, not Margot's, and that Conrad's guilty. But I never meant to say anything of the sort.'

'What I think you're suggesting,' Constance said, 'is that Mrs Barrow may have been blackmailing him because she'd somehow found out about his receiving stolen things, and when she came here on the visits that upset him so badly, she was making him pay her for her silence. Isn't that it?'

Julie tucked her hand back into her pocket. Her whole posture had changed. It had become rigidly challenging, as if she were prepared to defend herself against some on-slaught. Her frown looked angry rather than abstracted.

'Of course, I don't believe a word of it,' Constance said. 'What interests me is why you told me such a story.'

Julie did not reply.

'What did she buy when she came here?' Irene asked.

'Nothing,' Julie answered.

'Nothing ever?'

'No.'

'I mean, she wasn't collecting some special kind of thing and just didn't buy anything if Conrad didn't happen to have what she wanted in stock?'

'I told you, no.'

'Then perhaps Mr Greer got into a foul temper with her because he felt she was wasting his time,' Constance suggested. 'He's got a fairly volatile temper, hasn't he?'

Julie caught her breath again, managed to get rid of her frown and then even to smile a little.

'You know, that's what I used to think myself,' she said. 'It's just the atmosphere at the moment that makes one . . . Well, I've had such horrible thoughts going through my head ever since they found poor Jennifer's body. Its being found so near Conrad's house . . . No, there I go again, suggesting things. Please take no notice of what I've been saying. I'm simply not myself at the moment.'

'You aren't the only person who's pointed out that it wasn't far from the pool where they found your sister's body to Conrad's house,' Irene said. 'And there's the point that if he had nothing to do with her death, someone else had to get away from the pool and back to the village without being seen, unless it was a hitch-hiker who went in the opposite direction.'

'Who said anything about that?' Julie asked sharply.

'Kenneth Pauling.'

Julie raised her eyebrows, but said nothing. Constance stood up.

'We're wasting your time,' she said. 'If you'd like that plate, Irene—'

'No, no, no,' Irene broke in. 'I don't want it. I don't want anything.'

'Because you've got what you came for?' Julie asked.

She and Irene stared at one another, then Irene shook her head.

'More than we came for, really, but I'm not sure if it's any use.' She took Constance by the arm and guided her out of the shop.

They were in the car, on the way back to Constance's house, before either of them spoke again. Irene had a dreamy air as if her thoughts had drifted far away before Constance at last asked, 'What did you mean by saying we'd got more than we came for? It didn't seem to me we'd got much. But then I'm not sure why we went there at all.'

'Tell me something,' Irene said. 'You knew Mrs Barrow. I know she was a sick woman and perhaps wasn't quite her normal self, but can you imagine her being a blackmailer?'

'Didn't I tell Julie I didn't believe her?'

'That's what I thought. She was really a nice old lady, was she?'

'Very nice.'

'So the whole of what that Hyland woman told us about her was a lie. That's what I meant by saying we'd got more than we came for. We know now she's a liar.'

'But it may not all have been lies, you know,' Constance said.

'What do you mean?'

'Well, suppose it was quite true that Mrs Barrow used to come into the shop from time to time, bringing Colin with her and knowing, of course, that Conrad Greer was Colin's father, mightn't she have had some reason for coming to see him which had nothing to do with blackmail?'

'Such as?'

'Perhaps she just wanted to consult him about Colin's upbringing, or perhaps Greer contributed to Colin's keep and used to pay her then without its having anything to do with blackmail. I don't think the Barrows were specially well off.'

'Why wouldn't Greer pay them in their own home? He came there fairly often, didn't he?'

'Perhaps the Colonel didn't know of the arrangement. And if Greer could help them with Colin, it may have been welcome.'

'Or perhaps she never came at all.'

They had come to a halt in front of Constance's house. Constance looked into Irene's face which was turned away from her with an expression of deep thoughtfulness.

'Is that what you really think?' Constance asked.

'I'd be inclined to think so if I could think of a motive for her having told us that yarn,' Irene said.

'It would mean she's got some reason for wanting to get Greer into trouble, wouldn't it?' Constance said.

'Oh yes, that's what she was trying to do, that's obvious.'

'It's odd, because I'd been given the impression by the Colonel that she and Greer have probably had an affair going on over the years. It wouldn't be surprising if they had because they've worked together for a long time and she's an attractive woman.'

'Perhaps the trouble is that they haven't had an affair going on and she wants to take her revenge for that. On the other hand, suppose she's been blackmailing him herself and now wants to cover her tracks by getting people to believe Mrs Barrow was the troublemaker.'

'You believe Greer's a fence, do you, and has always known he was handling stolen property?'

'Oh yes, that's evident. What I'm not sure of is . . .' Irene stopped, opened the car door beside her and stepped out into the street.

Constance got out of the car too and locked it.

'What aren't you sure of?' she asked as they walked up the path to her front door.

'It's just that I've been wondering if I made a mistake yesterday,' Irene said. 'I was completely sure that Pauling was the murderer of his wife and Jennifer. I could feel it in my bones. But now—well, I'm not ready to say I was wrong, but I'm equally sure now that Greer's capable of murder. I don't say he committed these two particular murders in Long Meldon, but I'm sure he could have.'

'If luckily for him someone else hadn't done it first, you mean.'

'Now you're laughing at me,' Irene said. 'You always laugh at me. Why don't you ever take me seriously?'

'But often I do. It's just that sometimes I find it rather difficult.'

Constance had taken her latch-key out of her handbag and unlocked the door before them. It was true that she found it difficult to take seriously the feelings in Irene's bones and at the moment she would have been grateful if that morning the two of them had somehow stumbled on some solid evidence about the murders. But solid evidence was a job for the police, not for her and Irene, and the murders were not her business at all. She had told the police all that she knew about them and if there was anything more that they wanted from her they knew where to find her.

Stepping into the house, followed by Irene, she closed the door behind them and went to the kitchen to consider that ever recurring problem: what were they going to eat for lunch? She thought she would make omelettes and that before starting on them they might have some sherry.

It worried her, however, as she took sherry and glasses into the sitting-room where she found Irene slumped in a chair, staring broodingly before her, that some thought that in the morning had been clear to her had since eluded her. She knew that it had interested her briefly and that she had intended to think more about it later, but other things had distracted her and now she could not remember what it had been. Probably it had not been anything important. If it had been it would no doubt suddenly return to her while she was thinking about something else.

Holding her glass of sherry, she sat down, observing, 'I'm getting old.'

Irene did not appear to think it necessary to reply to this undeniable statement.

'My memory,' Constance went on, 'is not what it used to be.'

'I should say it's reasonably good, considering,' Irene said with some indifference, still plainly pursuing some line of thought of her own. 'I don't often catch you out.'

'But I catch myself out,' Constance said. 'Where there ought to be some quite clear idea in my mind there's sometimes just a blank. For instance, this morning . . .' But suddenly as she said that the lost thought came back to her. 'It's all right, I know what I wanted to say. It was about something Mrs Newcome said to me. Do you remember her telling us about seeing Greer in the village in the afternoon?'

'Yes.' Irene sipped her sherry. 'And I suppose she's told the police about it by now. Does it matter?'

'It's only that there's something a little odd about it,' Constance said. 'He came to Riverside in the afternoon, bringing the chessmen for Colin, and he came on foot. But when Mrs Newcome saw him he was in his car. So why didn't he come to Riverside by car on his way home? I know what you'll say. You'll say he'd forgotten to bring the chessmen with him and had to go home for them. But if he'd done that and had driven up the lane to his house, he'd have seen that Riverside was already crawling with policemen. And wouldn't it have been the normal thing for him to do then to stop and find out what was going on? But he didn't. He drove home, then quite a bit later arrived on foot, carrying the chessmen and making out that the sight of the police quite surprised him.'

'Doesn't that mean he didn't know the chessmen were stolen?'

'That's how it looks.'

'Actually I was just thinking about that trip of his to the village,' Irene said, 'but what I was wondering about is why he went there. Mrs Newcome told us he stopped at the café, went in and came out again almost immediately. I suppose because he found nobody there, so where was Julie when he did that? We know where Jennifer was. She was dead in the pool. And Mrs Crisp was in Bracklington with her husband, shopping. But where was Julie?'

'I telephoned the café early in the afternoon wanting to speak to Jennifer and Julie answered, so she was there then,' Constance said.

'You're sure of that?' Irene asked. 'I mean, that it was Julie?'

'Oh yes.'

'So it looks as if it wasn't Julie that he wanted to see. But if it was Jennifer, then he can't have been the person who pushed her into the pool. The fact that the pool's so near his house and that it would have been easier for him than for anyone else to get away from where she was left really doesn't mean anything. I believe my first feeling was right after all. It was Ken Pauling who did it. And he simply walked away and came back to the village and it just happened that nobody saw him. Unless, of course, somebody did see him and is keeping quiet about it.'

'Who are you thinking of?'

'Nobody in particular. It was just a thought.'

Irene did not explain herself further, for just then the doorbell rang.

It was Detective-Inspector Frayne who stood on the doorstep.

Constance invited him into the house, took him to the sitting-room and introduced him to Irene. She greeted him with a look of deep distrust. In the world in which she had been living for some years the police were normally regarded as the enemy. He did not seem to notice it and said that he was glad that her mother had her company at this very difficult time. But he did not seem much interested in her.

Taking the chair that Constance offered him while she herself sat down again, he said, 'You remember, Mrs Lawley, I asked you some questions about the set of fire irons in the Barrows' drawing-room?'

She nodded.

'And I told you,' he went on, 'that a shovel and tongs were there, but no poker.'

'Yes.'

'Well, we've found the poker. It was among some shrubs outside the back door of the house.'

'And you believe it was what was used to knock Jennifer Hyland unconscious.'

'We're sure of it. There are bloodstains and a few hairs on it. The hairs match hers and the blood is the same group as hers.'

'May I ask you then why you've taken the trouble to come and tell me about it?' Constance said. 'I don't mean I'm not interested, but I should have thought that from your point of view it would be a waste of time.'

'There's a question I want to ask you,' he said. 'Something I want to check up on. I believe on Saturday morning you went into the village to do some shopping, met Mr Pauling and had coffee with him in Jenny's Café.

'That's correct,' she said.

'But Miss Jennifer Hyland had already left the café before you went into it.'

'Yes, I saw her driving away.'

'Then who waited on you?'

'Jennifer's sister, Julie.'

'And when you left you went into the shop across the way and were there for some time.'

'I think I told you that, didn't I?'

'Yes, you did. But you were puzzled about why it seemed to have taken Jennifer Hyland so long to reach the Barrows' house. There was something like half an hour unaccounted for. Well, we have the answer to that now.'

'So have I. She spent it with Mrs Newcome, didn't she? She was here this morning and told us about it. She also told us about having seen Mr Greer in the village, going into the café and coming out of it again. She didn't seem to know if it could be of any importance, and nor did I, but I advised her to tell you about it. In fact, I gave her a lift to the police station.'

'So she told me and that's partly why I'm here. Assuming that Miss Hyland didn't arrive at Riverside until a short time before you got back there, because of her having spent some time with Mrs Newcome, there was time before she arrived for someone to get from the village to the house and witness the murders by the boy Colin and add another of his own to them, even if he'd been in the café with you until the time when you went into the grocer's.'

'You're talking of Mr Pauling.'

'Of course he is,' Irene said with a touch of weariness in her tone, as if she thought this a matter about which too much had been said already. 'I know you can't arrest him till you've something solid to go on, but you know he's guilty, don't you? There's just one thing that puzzles me.'

He appeared for the first time to take an interest in her.

'Yes?' he said.

'Why didn't he shoot Jennifer, if he wanted to get rid of her? Why did he take to using a poker?'

'For a very simple reason, Miss Lawley,' he said. 'The gun was empty.'

'I don't understand,' she said. 'Colin shot his grandparents and himself and then Pauling shot Margot—that's four bullets. Doesn't a gun hold more bullets than that?'

'In this case, six,' he answered. 'But we've found two bullets embedded in the wall of the drawing-room to one side of the fireplace, near to where the Colonel's body was. Colin, it would appear, was not a very good shot. He wasted two bullets. So when the other character, whoever it was, came in, found himself face to face with Margot Pauling and shot her, he was using the last bullet in the gun.'

'So when he discovered there was a witness to this, he had to use something else to get rid of her, and as it happens it was the poker.' Irene sounded excited. 'And he couldn't leave her just lying there, could he? That would have shown you at once that there'd been another murderer in the room besides Colin.'

'Exactly.'

'Dragging her body out to the car and then pushing it

into the pool must have taken some strength,' she said. 'Pauling's a fairly powerful man, I should say.'

'You've met him, then?' he asked.

'Oh yes.'

'And you're convinced he murdered his wife and Jennifer Hyland?'

For once Irene looked a little embarrassed.

'It's just an idea of mine,' she said. 'If I explained why I think it, you wouldn't understand me.'

'Why not try me?' he suggested.

She shook her head. 'It's nothing that would interest you. I mean, unless you've had some experience yourself of finding out you just know something, you can't explain it.'

'But I've often had that experience,' he said, 'only it generally turns out I've been wrong. Naturally it's just the times when I've been right that I like to remember. But perhaps your intuitions are more efficient than mine.'

He must be basically a kind man, Constance thought, even if his profession had hardened him.

He turned back to her. 'So you and Mr Pauling were waited on in the café by Julie Hyland, so you can give her an alibi.'

'Julie Hyland—an alibi!' Constance exclaimed. 'Have you really been thinking she could have been the murderer?'

'We've been thinking of everybody,' he said, 'even the butcher and the baker and the candlestick-maker. The grocer, you may be interested to hear, can confirm that you came into his shop at about eleven o'clock and spent a longish time there.'

'So you've even been checking up on me!'

'Oh yes.'

'But I believe that if I had hit someone on the head with a poker, I'd hardly have made a dent. I'm reasonably strong, but not up to knocking a person out. And I could never have dragged the poor girl's body to the car.'

'And you hadn't time to do it, which is perhaps the most

convincing reason why you can't be under suspicion.' He stood up. 'It's an annoying thing, in view of the fact that he may well be guilty, that Mr Pauling has disappeared. He walked out of the Green Dragon yesterday evening and hasn't been seen since. He may be a person who got on to a bus into Bracklington, but the identification isn't positive. However, we'll catch up with him without much difficulty, I imagine, but it's a waste of valuable time and very irritating. Well, thank you, Mrs Lawley, and you, Miss Lawley.'

He did not wait as Constance got hurriedly to her feet to go to the front door and let him out, but turned quickly, left the sitting-room and let himself out of the house.

Constance sank down in her chair and reached for her sherry.

'So it looks as if you may have been right after all,' she said.

'That Pauling must be guilty because he's disappeared?' Irene said.

'Well, why else should he go?'

'I can think of all sorts of reasons though they don't affect my view of him. One, he might just have wanted to get home to Australia. Two, that he knew of some evidence against someone else, probably Conrad Greer, realized he's in danger because of it and got out while he could. Three, he didn't much like the Green Dragon and he's gone to look for some better hotel. Four, he's been murdered and his body hasn't been found yet. Five, he's found he can't live with his conscience and has committed suicide. Six—'

'Stop!' Constance cried. 'You still think he's guilty.'

'I'm not as sure of that as I was, since meeting Conrad Greer. If I hadn't already met Pauling, I'd be sure Greer was the murderer.'

'Of Mrs Barrow, as Julie suggested.'

'Of course not. That was all moonshine. If anyone was blackmailing Greer, I'd guess it was Julie herself, or perhaps she was just going shares with him in the proceeds of his receiving and wanted to put all the blame she could on him, just to clear herself, as the thing seemed to be coming out. But you didn't tell that man Frayne anything about what Julie said. Was that because you didn't believe it?'

'I think it was really because I was thinking of something else,' Constance said. 'It's something that's been puzzling me, though I haven't really thought about it. Look, what the police believe is that Jennifer went to Riverside to deliver Colin's cake and that she arrived just in time to see someone take the gun that Colin had dropped and shoot someone with it, probably Margot. But what would you have done yourself if you'd seen a thing like that? Would you have stayed around to be hit on the head with a poker?'

'I'd have bolted for my life,' Irene said.

Constance nodded. 'So should I, unless I was feeling very brave and dashed into the dining-room, where there's a telephone, and dialled 999. But I think I'd have bolted, jumped into my car and driven off to the police as fast as I could.'

Irene looked at her uncertainly. 'But she didn't do that, so what do you think really happened?'

'The only thing I can think of is that the murderer, as soon as he realized she was there, threatened her with the gun, which she didn't know was empty, then snatched up the poker and hit her with it.'

'But didn't hit her hard enough to kill her with it. He only knocked her unconscious, then carried her out to her car and drove off to the pool. Of course he had to remove her from the scene, but why didn't he kill her outright, then carry her out?'

'Because he was in a hurry. He knew I'd be getting back to the house soon and wanted to get away before I arrived.'

'And who would have known that?'

'I suppose Pauling.'

Irene gave a hollow little laugh. 'So you're coming round to my view after all. You've taken your time about it, looking for so-called solid evidence instead of just trusting to your instincts, which is really so much wiser. But at least you agree with me now. You really do, don't you, Mum?'

'The only trouble is, I don't think anyone could call that really solid evidence,' Constance replied. 'There may have been several other people who'd heard I was working for the Barrows and saw me in the village and knew for sure I'd be getting back soon. Conrad Greer may have seen me. Julie did. Mrs Crisp did. Mrs Newcome perhaps.'

'It's got to be someone strong,' Irene said. 'Strong enough to carry Jennifer's body to the car. And you've said yourself Julie has an alibi. So was it Pauling or Greer?'

Constance stood up. 'I think I'll go and get the lunch,' she said. 'We'll never get anywhere, talking like this.'

She went out to the kitchen to make the omelettes.

She was glad that when lunch was over Irene found a book on one of Constance's bookshelves that she appeared inclined to read. She settled down on the sofa with her feet up and showed no desire to go on talking. Curious as to what might interest Irene at such a time, Constance glanced over her shoulder to see what the book was and saw that it was an old copy that she had forgotten that she possessed of Stevenson's *Travels with a Donkey*. Constance remembered that Irene had spoken of going travelling with Samuel on bicycles or on foot and wondered if it had occurred to her that a donkey might be a more interesting form of transport than either.

It did not seem unlike her. She seemed deeply absorbed in the book, for which Constance was grateful. She felt too restless to be able to read herself, but she had some knitting which had been lying about in the room for some time and to which she occasionally added a few rows, and she thought that doing this now might be calming. But she had no sooner picked it up and sat down with it than the telephone rang.

'Mrs Lawley?' It was the voice of Mrs Jay from the

Bracklington Helpers. 'I've been reading the terrible news about the house I sent you to last week. My dear, I can't tell you how sorry I feel to have got you involved in such a dreadful thing. I know in our work we can sometimes run into very strange situations, but you aren't really involved in all this, are you?'

'If you mean, am I suspected of the murders or have I been helping the police with their inquiries, well, no, I don't think I've helped them much and I don't think I'm suspected of anything,' Constance replied. 'But I was thinking of ringing you up to ask if I'm going to be paid for the full week I was engaged for, or only for the time I actually spent at Riverside, because of course I haven't done the full time. We can forget the whole thing if you like, because I certainly haven't done a normal amount of work.'

'Of course you'll be paid for the full time,' Mrs Jay said. 'I'm sure what you've been through has been much more wearing than the hardest kind of work. But you're all right, are you? I mean, the shock hasn't been too great for you. Do you think you'd be up to doing another job?'

'No, oh no, I couldn't possibly,' Constance said swiftly. 'I'm sorry, but I just feel I've got to stay at home very quietly.'

'I understand, of course, I was just hoping . . . Such a nice young couple, you know, and they really need help.'

'The Barrows were a very nice old couple, but all the help I could give them didn't do much.'

'This is different. The poor girl had a fall and broke three ribs. She did it falling out of bed, would you believe it? Such an odd accident. And they've a dear little boy—'

'I'm not going anywhere again where there are children, Mrs Jay,' Constance interrupted.

'Oh, that doesn't sound like you, Mrs Lawley,' Mrs Jay said. 'Of course I know you must need a rest and I won't press you, but if you should change your mind . . . The fact is, we seem to have had an epidemic of accidents and operations and illnesses of all kinds, and we don't seem to have any spare helpers at the moment, and I do so hate refusing people. Well, perhaps I can find someone else. Take care of yourself, won't you? Do you know if the police have any idea who killed the girl they found in the pond?'

'If they have, they haven't confided in me,' Constance said.

'But they believe it was because she witnessed those murders in the house, don't they? That's what it said in the paper. You didn't actually witness anything yourself, did you?'

'Nothing at all. I just walked into a room and found four dead bodies there.'

'Terrible, terrible! Well, as I said, take care of yourself. I'm so glad you didn't actually witness anything. And I suppose nobody can think you did it.'

Constance said firmly, 'Nobody,' and Mrs Jay said goodbye and rang off.

Constance returned to her knitting. But as she picked it up she scowled at it, partly because she felt confused about the pattern, but also because Mrs Jay's concern for her safety had suddenly made her wonder if in fact it was possible that whoever had struck so devastatingly at Riverside could believe for a moment that she had seen or knew something more than she actually did.

And did she in fact know something more than she realized?

Her mouth took on a hard line as she tried to concentrate on the complicated pattern that she had chosen for her knitting, mistakenly, for she was not really an expert knitter, while at the same time attempting to discover why she should have the uncomfortable feeling that she knew something that was eluding her grasp. She had one of her attacks once more of feeling that her memory was not what it had been. But was there really anything to remember? She might be simply the victim of strain and weariness which left her feeling guiltily inadequate to cope with the situation in which she was trapped.

She knitted on doggedly for some time. Then suddenly she said, 'Irene, I told that Inspector a lie.'

Irene grunted. Her book was lying flat on her stomach and she was sound asleep.

Constance raised her voice. 'Irene!'

'What? Oh yes—did you say something?' Irene blinked at her.

'I said I told Frayne a lie.'

'That's funny,' Irene said. 'You don't often tell lies. You're a very truthful person.'

'I didn't mean to do it. It was sheer stupidity on my part.'

'Well, what was it?'

'I said that Julie Hyland waited on Pauling and me when we had coffee in Jenny's Café, and that gave her an alibi.'

'Yes.'

'But she didn't. She took our order, but it was Mrs Crisp who brought the coffee and later on our bill. Perhaps Mrs Crisp can give Julie an alibi. She may know that she was out in the kitchen all the morning, but all I can say myself is that she took our order and then disappeared.'

'Are you saying that Julie murdered Margot and then her sister?'

'I'm only saying that perhaps she could have done it.'

'But she couldn't have known there'd be a gun lying around handy, could she? That's one of the things that's been worrying me about Pauling. How did he know there'd be a gun there? It looks as if Julie, if she did go up to the house while you were having coffee and then doing your shopping, can't have had any intention of committing murder.'

'I know. All the same, I think I'm going to go along to the police station and tell them I've misled them.'

'What, now?'

'Yes,' Constance said, putting down her knitting and standing up.

'Oh dear,' Irene said, 'I'm so sleepy.'

'You needn't come.'

'Oh, I'll come. I feel happier, keeping an eye on you.'

'Of course I'm remembering that it would have taken someone with a good deal of strength to get Jennifer into her car and then push her into the pool.'

'Are you thinking about the Biedermeier?'

'The what?' Constance asked.

'The Biedermeier chest in Conrad Greer's shop. Didn't you notice it?'

'You don't mean you think it was stolen? I should think it was too big. Most of the things taken from that house in Granwich were probably quite small, which the burglar could carry away with him.'

Irene swung her legs to the ground. 'One does hear of furniture vans arriving outside houses where the owners have gone away and clearing the places out. The neighbours don't take any notice because they think the owners are simply moving away. But if that chest was stolen, I don't suppose it would have been put into the shop window. It would more probably be on its way to Australia by now.'

'Why did you mention it then?'

'Oh, just a thought.'

'Well, if we're going to the police station, the sooner we get going the better.'

Constance felt that even if what she had to tell Frayne was a matter of no interest to him—if, for instance, Mrs Crisp had been able to say that Julie had been in the kitchen of the café all the morning—she would still feel easier in her mind when she had corrected what she had told him before.

She picked up her handbag, took her car keys out of it, went to the front door and opened it.

Kenneth Pauling had just got out of a taxi at the gate and came walking up the path towards her.

CHAPTER 9

Constance paused in the doorway, then made a gesture, inviting him to come in. She said nothing. Irene did not say anything either. She looked at him with an intent, penetrating gaze while he hardly looked at her. Making a fist of one hand, he raised it and stared at it as if there were something that he felt he ought to be able to do with it, though he was not sure what.

After a moment Constance said, 'Where have you been? The police have been looking for you.'

'I've only been to London,' he said. 'I wanted to see an old friend of mine, someone I knew before I went to Australia. A solicitor. I saw him this morning. I wanted his help in case I get arrested for this thing. It seems I may be going to inherit the Barrows' money, which gives me a kind of motive. Also I wanted him to take over my affairs. I want to get back to Australia as soon as they'll let me go, but if there's anything for me to inherit, I don't want to throw it away.'

'Do you think you're going to be arrested?' Constance asked.

He shrugged his shoulders. 'I think anything could happen, but I'm not running away from it.'

'That's what the police thought you were doing,' she said.

'I've come back again, haven't I?'

Irene was still eyeing him with doubt and suspicion in her glance.

'But why just here?' she asked. 'What do you want with my mother?'

'Ah, that's what I'd better explain,' he said. 'You remember our having coffee on Saturday morning, Mrs Lawley?'

'Yes, of course,' she said.

'Do you remember that Julie Hyland took our order that morning, but afterwards we were waited on by a little woman in a pink overall?'

'Mrs Crisp,' she said. 'Yes.'

'Well, I had a talk with Mrs Crisp yesterday evening before I left for London and I asked her if Julie Hyland had in fact been in the café all the morning, or if she'd left it. Mrs Crisp said she hadn't seen her and had had to manage on her own.'

'It's a funny thing, but Irene and I were just on our way to the police to tell them about that,' Constance said. 'I mean, that the alibi I'd given Julie didn't hold water. But I haven't spoken to Mrs Crisp, so I didn't know if perhaps Julie had spent the rest of the morning in the kitchen.

'She didn't,' he said. 'And I came here to ask you to come to the police with me to support me when I tell them about Julie disappearing from the café after she'd taken our orders.'

'Yes, of course, I'll do that,' Constance said. 'But why do you think she did that? Where did she go?'

'My belief is she went up to Greer's house to have a talk with him about Margot and got him to go to Riverside to tell her that the old affair wasn't going to start again. I think Julie was very frightened that it might. She'd had an affair with him herself for years but she may have known that the one he'd had with Margot all that time ago had meant far more to him than she ever had, particularly in view of their having had the child, whom that man really loved. And Julie told him that you were in the village, so you wouldn't be around to overhear them talking, and she guessed the old people wouldn't eavesdrop because they were probably still hoping, for the child's sake, that his affair with Margot could be patched up, and she said that if he didn't do what she wanted she was going to tip the police off that he'd been receiving stolen property for years. He was pretty much in her power. So he went along and walked into the house just as Colin started his campaign of murder. And what happened then . . .' He had dropped his fist and his gaze was fastened with a strange, sightless brilliance on Constance's face. 'I don't know what happened,' he added lamely. 'It's possible he and Margot were on the terrace, talking. I believe they've deduced she was out there by the cigarette stubs in the ashtray on the table. And the two of them may have gone running into the room when the shooting started and Greer tried to get the gun away from Colin and somehow shot Margot by accident. I don't want to blame a man who's innocent in his way . . .' He paused, then added explosively, 'But I don't believe it! I believe he shot Margot in cold blood!'

'And Jennifer walked in on the scene and so had to be silenced and disposed of.'

'Yes.' He rubbed a hand across his eyes. He looked exceedingly tired, as if he had not slept much during his night in London. 'God, why didn't I go up to the house myself that morning? I nearly did after we'd separated, you know. I thought of going there and trying to persuade Margot to come home with me. Perhaps I'd have been too late even if I'd done that, but I might have saved the girl. However, it's not much good thinking about that now. Will you come to the police with me?'

'Yes, but really this is all very hypothetical, isn't it?' Constance said. 'If you're right that Julie was in Greer's house at the time of the murders, how did she get home again without being seen? She was in the café when I telephoned in the afternoon.'

'But that's easy,' Irene said. She had not taken her eyes off Pauling's face from the time when he had come into the room. She looked as if she were trying to find out what was going on in his brain simply by using her gaze to bore into his skull. 'She came in Greer's car. Do you remember how Mrs Newcome told us about seeing him drive up to the café just before she went into the grocer's opposite? Of course

Julie was hidden in the car. And he went quickly into the café to make certain Mrs Crisp wasn't there, then at a moment when the street was empty Julie scrambled out of the car and shot into the café. And Greer turned round the notice on the door to say it was closed and drove away.'

'You might think she could have walked home in an ordinary way without all that complication after she'd sent Greer off to talk to Margot,' Constance said, 'except that I suppose she wanted to hear what he'd got to say when he got back, and when she did hear what had actually happened she was frightened of becoming involved herself and made him take her home in the way you say.'

'Are we going to the police?' Pauling said.

'Come along.' Constance led the way out and they packed themselves into the Mini.

However, when they arrived at the police station and asked for Inspector Frayne the duty sergeant informed them that both he and Sergeant Randall were out on a case and that he knew nothing about when they might be likely to return. For a few minutes they argued about what they should do. None of them wanted to discuss the situation with a stranger who perhaps might be well-informed about the Riverside case, but on the other hand might need to have most of it explained to him. They did not know how fully the members of a local police force kept each other informed. It was surely sense, Constance said, to leave a message for Mr Frayne, asking him to get in touch with her as soon as he returned to the police station, or even before, as she was sure the sergeant here would be able to communicate with him immediately by one of those clever radio devices so many people have now. Then the three of them could go back to her house and have some tea and wait for the Inspector to arrive. Irene for once appeared to have no opinion. She had given up her deep study of Pauling's expression and when Constance asked her what she thought they should do, only muttered in reply, 'The

Biedermeier . . . Yes, of course.' Then she looked as if she
wished that she had not said that. But Pauling was quite
sure of what they should do.

'I'm going to Greer's house,' he said. 'If you don't want
to take me I'll get a taxi.' He turned to the sergeant. 'Can
I get a taxi here?'

'Sometimes,' the sergeant answered not very encourag-
ingly.

'It isn't far to walk,' Constance said.

'All right, I'll walk.'

'But of course we'll drive you up there,' Irene said. 'I
suppose you want to get your hands on Greer. I'm sure I
should if I were you. Believing what you do, I mean.'

'Don't you believe me?' he asked.

Instead of answering she chewed the tip of a finger.

'Let's go, then,' Constance said, and led the way back to
her car.

They did not talk as they drove to Conrad Greer's house.
Constance could sense the extreme tension in Pauling, who
was sitting beside her. When they passed Riverside she saw
a group of people gathered at the gate. Sightseers, she
supposed, and was glad that there was a constable there to
stop them going in. She drove on to the house beyond and
there saw that there was a police car in the road in front of
it. The three of them got out of the Mini and with Pauling
leading them, went up to the door on which he pounded
with a heavy iron knocker.

There was no answer. After a moment Pauling knocked
again and there was still no answer. When he had waited
impatiently a little longer he grasped the door handle and
turned it. The door swung open. The sound of voices came
to them from one of the rooms inside, but these ceased as
Pauling, Constance and Irene entered the house. Pauling
strode in the direction of the room from which the voices
had come and Constance and Irene followed him.

The room was the one in which Conrad Greer had shown

Colonel Barrow the chessmen. Greer was there and so were Inspector Frayne and Sergeant Randall and a uniformed constable.

Seeing the intruders, Randall observed, 'Christ!' It seemed that their appearance just then was a little more than he could tolerate.

Greer said, 'Oh, it's you.' It seemed to be a matter of indifference to him.

'Are you under arrest?' Pauling demanded aggressively.

'Mr Greer's helping us with our inquiries,' Frayne said with irony in his tone.

'Oh yes, I'm under arrest,' Greer said. 'They were just speaking the words of that terrible warning when you knocked.' He turned to Frayne. 'Would you care to repeat it? You were in the middle of it when they came.'

Though his voice had a languid flatness there was a look of desperation on his face. His eyes seemed to have sunk deep into his head. His mouth was a tight, hard line.

Wearily, as if the subject had begun to bore him, Frayne said, 'Conrad Greer, I am a police officer and I arrest you for the receiving of property knowing it to be stolen, and I have to tell you that anything you say may be taken down and used as evidence at your trial.'

'Receiving stolen property!' Pauling shouted. 'Is that all? What about the murder of my wife?'

'I didn't murder her,' Greer remarked in the same lackadaisical tone. 'Yes, I've been handling stolen property and shipping it to you in Australia. And Margot knew it, if you didn't. I'm pleading guilty to that as they've already arrested the bastard who's been bringing the stuff to me for the last two or three years and he's spilled his guts about it. But I haven't murdered anyone. However, it wouldn't surprise me if you had.'

Pauling's face turned a dark red. 'If I could get hold of you—'

'Please, Mr Pauling,' Frayne interrupted. 'Let's take this

quietly. We have no evidence at the moment that Mr Greer
murdered Jennifer Hyland or your wife. Perhaps you can
help us obtain some. Did you suppose your wife knew of
Conrad Greer's exporting stolen property to Australia and
that he had any reason to fear, when she arrived here, that
she meant to expose him, or possibly to blackmail him?'

'Certainly not,' Pauling said. 'I don't believe she knew
anything about it.'

'Did you?'

'Did I know about this racket of his? I did not. I assumed
she was dealing with him because they were old friends.'

'Friends?' Frayne said as if he found the word a curious
one. 'It wasn't because she could get the merchandise
unusually cheaply from him?'

'I've never heard of such a thing,' Pauling said. 'And
poor Margot's dead. You can't badger her with questions.'

Frayne nodded sadly. 'True.'

'You know, Mr Frayne,' Irene said suddenly, 'what you
need at the moment is some solid evidence.'

Constance looked at her in astonishment. That Irene
could consider solid evidence as more important at the
moment than her own intuitions about the case seemed so
unlikely as to be almost incredible. Then Constance realized
that Irene might not be doing so. She might simply be
pandering to what she regarded as an almost whimsical
need in other people for plain, hard facts. Her own beliefs
would remain paramount to her, but she did not mind
helping the less gifted to understand them. But it appeared
that they had altered since she had last talked about them.

'There's a Biedermeier chest of drawers in the window
of Conrad Greer's shop,' she said. 'That's solid enough,
isn't it?'

Frayne gave a slight shake of his head. 'I'm afraid I don't
understand you.'

'I mean, it's solid and heavy,' she said. 'It's an elegant-
looking thing, but it's really quite heavy, yet when my

mother and I went into the Greer shop this morning Conrad
Greer and Julie Hyland between them were moving that
chest into the window. And what's your sole reason for
believing Julie Hyland didn't murder her sister? Isn't it only
that she wouldn't have been strong enough to handle her
body, get it into the car and then into the pool? But if a
person's learnt how to handle heavy weights properly they
can move all sorts of things. Have you ever watched removal
men handling furniture? Sometimes they're quite small men,
yet between them they can carry great wardrobes and things
like that up a couple of flights of stairs. And Julie had had
lots of practice in the shop, so she could have carried her
sister quite easily.'

Constance could not stop herself interrupting. 'But why
should she have done that?'

'Don't you understand?' Irene said. 'Julie was hopelessly
in love with Conrad Greer. She had been for years, even
before he had that affair with Margot and the birth of Colin.
And she jumped to the conclusion when she heard Margot
was here that she was going to try to get him back. So on
Saturday morning, after she'd taken your order for coffee,
she suddenly thought she'd go up to Riverside and tell
Margot that she'd better not try to take Conrad away from
her. She'd no idea then of committing murder, because of
course she didn't know that there'd be a gun available, but
she and Margot sat on the terrace, talking and we'll never
know what they talked about, but perhaps Margot mocked
her, saying she could get Conrad away if she chose, or
threatened that she was going to expose his illegal dealing,
but somehow she must have made Julie angry and then the
shooting started and there were three dead people and a
gun on the floor. So she shot Margot. It must have seemed
such an easy way out of her difficulties. But at just that
moment Jennifer walked in. One of the odd things that's
puzzled us, hasn't it, is that Jennifer didn't either bolt for
her life or rush to dial 999? She seems just to have stood

there, looking on and perhaps talking, and wasn't that natural if it was her own sister whom she saw committing murder?'

She paused at the sound of the front door being opened. Julie Hyland walked into the room.

Irene looked at her blankly as if the real Julie were someone whom, all the time she had been talking, she had never really envisaged. She could easily deal with a figure that existed in her imagination, but flesh and blood upset her. She went a little pale.

'There she is,' she said uneasily after the brief silence that followed Julie's entrance into the room. 'I'm sure she'll confess if you show you know what she's done.'

Julie stood there only for a moment, taking in the scene before her, then with the light of panic glittering wildly in her eyes, she whirled and raced from the room. Frayne snapped out a word and the sergeant and the constable plunged after her. Constance heard the sound of Julie's car starting up in the road before she heard the police car. But she did not think that Julie would get far.

Frayne seemed unexcited. He looked at Irene and said, 'You were saying?'

'Well, I've said nearly all of it,' Irene replied, 'except that Julie decided she'd got to get rid of Jennifer before her conscience got the better of her and she went to the police. So as Jennifer started walking out to her car, Julie picked up the poker and hit her on the head. If she'd been really strong instead of just skilled at carrying things I suppose she'd have killed her on the spot, but actually she only managed to knock her unconscious. Then she drove her up to the pool and drowned her there. After that, instead of walking back to the village, knowing she might be seen on the way, she came here and told Conrad Greer what she'd done. And he hid her here till just after the lunch-hour, when he knew the village would be quiet and Mrs Crisp would have left the café, and he drove her in and she was there in time to take my mother's telephone call. About his own visit to Riverside and the chessmen, well, I think he felt he'd got to find out what was going on there, and taking the chessmen seemed a good excuse and he never dreamt they'd be easily identified as stolen. He's the kind of person who expects to be able to get away with everything.'

'Thank you, Miss Lawley,' the Inspector said. 'That's very suggestive.'

'Suggestive!' she exclaimed. 'Don't you believe me?'

'One's belief, unfortunately, is rarely enough to secure a conviction,' he replied. 'But as I said, it's suggestive. Mr Greer, do you wish to make any comment?'

'I'm not saying anything,' Conrad Greer said.

Frayne nodded, as if that were naturally to be expected.

'Then I'll just telephone for another car,' he said. 'It's time we were getting back to the station.'

That evening Constance picked up a packet of fish and chips from the shop round the corner from the house, put it into the oven to keep warm while she and Irene drank some whisky, then when they had had their supper Constance rang up Mrs Jay, whose home number she happened to know, and told her that after all, if Mrs Jay had not already fixed them up with someone else, she would be glad to help the nice young couple with the dear little boy and would go to them next day if necessary.

Why she did it she was not sure. She was feeling more tired, she believed, than she had ever felt in her life, yet if she could be useful to someone who was in trouble, she thought that it might help to lift the load of depression from her more effectively than sitting at home in an empty house. She was going to miss Irene who would be going home to her new flat next day, she supposed. In spite of the fact that while she was telephoning to Mrs Jay a strange and dreadful noise filled the house and she knew that it was Irene practising on the French horn and that too much of it might drive her mad, she wished that the girl were staying for a little longer.

She had just sat down once more in her sitting-room and picked up her knitting, not sure if she was really in a state to concentrate on the pattern, when the doorbell rang. Wearily, she went to answer it.

A small man stood there. He was about fifty, had sandy hair which was beginning to recede from his forehead, which was high, with deep lines of thought across it and bushy eyebrows above eyes of a clear, intense blue. His nose was short and turned up a little, his mouth was wide and smiled with singular gentleness and charm. He had a slight paunch and was wearing a wind-cheater and old, baggy trousers.

She knew what he was going to say before he said it.

'I'm Samuel,' he said.

She felt sure that she was going to like him.